Always Eat When You Are Hungry

TradShack

Copyright © August 2024. All rights reserved.

Leonard John hereby asserts and gives notice of his rights under the Copyright, Design and Patents Act, 1988 to be identified as the author of this work.

Always Eat When You Are Hungry is a work of fiction. Any resemblance to actual events or persons, living or dead, is entirely coincidental

No part of this book may be reproduced, or stored in a retrieval system, or transmitted in any form or by any means, electronic, mechanical, photocopying, recording, or otherwise, without express written permission of the publisher.

First published August 2024

Adult rating (contains strong language)

Cover design by www.tradshack.com

Published by www.tradshack.com

Act 1

Chapter 1

The Stranger

The stranger's arrival at Caister Holiday Park was as unexpected as the storm that lashed the Norfolk coast that morning. Francesca Lopresti wrestled the wonky-wheeled, cast iron trolley between the dining tables, mindful that on each one was a water-filled glass vase of flowers freshly picked that morning by the children of the kitchen staff. Picking flowers for the tables was a sought-after job, and only those children deemed to have been 'good' were awarded the task. Some of the arrangements were so bizarre they made her smile. One arrangement in particular deserved closer inspection. Surely that's a weed, not a flower? Anyway, it matters not, she concluded. Breakfast was in less than 30 minutes, and she had work to do. She could see the usual early-bird holidaymakers gathering outside the main door of the dining hall, shivering, peering through the salty, sand-encrusted glass, hoping for an early breakfast. The weather had not been kind to the campers this morning, nor to the flower pickers, but this was Norfolk, not Italy and anyway, everybody here was either on annual holiday or was working for the Caister management team, so sunshine and rain were tolerated in equal measure.

Despite the trolley's attempts to sabotage her work and a few minor collisions, Francesca set out the final table settings at the sea view end of the hall. Making sure all the flower vases, cutlery placements and table number plaques were correctly in place, she undid the ties of her apron, pulled the halter over her head and, folding it neatly, stowed it away on the trolley's lower shelf where it stayed until the lunchtime shift. When she straightened up, she was confronted by the face of a tall, long-haired stranger, hands cupped around his forehead, peering through the glass and smiling at her.

'Can ye open up an' let us in child? It's feckin' freezing out here.' Francesca instinctively raised her hand to her face, startled by the sudden appearance of this stranger. His long, dark hair was plastered to his face, dripping with rainwater that trickled down his cheeks and onto his collar. She hesitated momentarily, unsure whether to comply with his request or wait for her supervisor's approval. Francesca pointed to the wall clock. 'Non, non signore, too soon, too soon. You come back eight-thirty. Breakfast ready then.'

'I'm not here for a feed child, I have messages to conduct. Open the door please. This is not a social call.'

'Non, non signore. No key, no key.'

'Well, go and get the key then, child. I'm getting feckin' blown away out here, aye.'

Francesca backed away from the window pointing to the kitchen doors. 'I get boss.'

'You do that child.'

The stranger made his way to the main door, turning his collar against the North Sea wind. As he approached, a key rattled in the lock, and the door swung open.

The keyholder eyed the stranger with suspicion. 'Si signore. What can I do for you?'

'You can let me in, out of this feckin' weather, for starters.' The stranger shoved the keyholder aside and tore off his overcoat shaking it with a fury. He threw it on a dining table knocking a flower vase to the floor, smashing it to pieces.

'Che palle!' cried the keyholder hands held above his head. 'Look, signore, look what you do.'

The stranger grabbed the keyholder by his lapel and frog-marched him to the centre of the dining room, away from the prying eyes of the early birds. 'Never mind the feckin' vase. I'm here for one thing only. I'm going to ask yeez a simple question. How the rest of your day pans out will depend on the answer ye give. D'youse understand me, boyo?'

The keyholder nodded. 'Si signore.'

The stranger reached into his pocket and produced a crumpled photograph, holding it in front of the keyholder's face. 'Ok then. Where do I find Tommy Baker?'

The stranger's eyes glinted with cold determination, making the keyholder's blood run cold. With a sinking feeling, he realised that Tommy's continued good health depended on his next words.

Chapter 2

Easter Sunday

If you had taken a stroll down Tooley Street on that warm Easter Sunday afternoon of April 18th, 1954, you would have found that the street, usually echoing with the rumble of trucks and the shouts of dockworkers, was instead filled with the gentle buzz of celebration. At the St. John's Tavern on the corner of Weaver's Lane, its doors thrown open wide to welcome the spring air, a hive of activity spilled out onto the sun-bathed pavement. A group of men stood with their pints in hand, ties loosened, and jackets draped over their arms, basking in the unseasonable warmth, the clink of glasses and the occasional roar of collective laughter punctuating the constant murmur of voices. Work at the docks was a good two days away, and since none of the patrons had any intention of attending Holy Communion, the St. John's Tavern seemed the more fitting place to gather.

So it happened on this sunny afternoon that Police Constable 'Uncle' George Turner from the Tower Bridge Police Station rode his standard police bicycle along Tooley Street until he reached the sanctuary of Potters Fields Park, where he left his bike leaning against what remained of the cast iron railings. Removing his police helmet, he took out his handkerchief to dry the damp leather headband and took a seat on the park bench, pausing from his duties for a moment, taking in the sights and sounds of a resting community. At the edge of the park stood Antonio with his ice cream cart, cranking the handle of his barrel organ, its tinkling, nostalgic melody drifting across the scene, capturing the very essence of this perfect spring day, its notes dancing on the warm breeze and mixing with the rustling leaves of the park's trees.

George retrieved his pocketbook and pencil. He inserted the pencil's tip into the binding, and a cigarette appeared from the other side. Shifting on the bench, he rummaged in his trouser pocket for his Ronson. After a quick glance to see if anyone was watching, he lit the cigarette. Two young women in summer dresses waved hello. With his usual polite manners, George tipped his finger to his forehead while cradling his Woodbine in his other hand, now held low and out of sight.

'You be careful now Uncle,' shrieked one of the girls, loud enough so anyone within a five-mile radius could hear. 'Them fags ain't good for your 'ealth!'

George glanced around, hoping nobody heard the cheeky little mare. Then, laughing out loud, he spluttered an immense plume of white smoke high into the air, his cover blown. The girls, checking to see if George was intent on pursuit, made their escape skipping and giggling along Queen Elizabeth Street. The Woodbine resumed its rightful place, and taking a final drag, George rubbed out the hot tip with his fingers and stuffed the remainder into his lapel pocket along with his pencil and notebook.

'Right,' he said to himself, and standing to brush the flecks of cigarette ash from his trousers, he donned his helmet in preparation for police business. 'Let's go and see what those gentlemen in the St John's Tavern are up to'. And so, with the grace and poise of an old head looking forward to some unchallenging, adolescent banter, with one hand on the saddle, the other checking his police whistle was close to hand, George ushered his bicycle towards the merriment.

As George approached, one or two younger-looking members of the entourage glanced apprehensively at each other before shuffling back inside the bar. George clanked his bicycle handlebars against the frosted glass window, and removing his helmet, he entered the arena.

'Oy, Oy! Cunsternoon Afterble!' The place erupted with cheers and laughter.

George glared at Frankie Miller. 'Shah-tup, you cheeky little git! Does your mother know you're on the piss again?'

'Oooohhhhh!' declared the revellers.

'Please don't nick me George,' Frankie cried. 'I ain't had no dinner yet!'

More uproar.

'I wouldn't waste the lead in my pencil on you, you tedious little tit'. The room erupted once more. Smiling from ear to ear George made his way to the bar. 'What's the occasion?'

Ken, the Landlord, threw his towel over his shoulder. 'A newborn George! Lizzie's given birth. A little boy. Called 'im James, so I gather.'

'Ah yeah, Lizzie Butler. Is she OK?'

'She's fine by all account. Joyce went up to Guys on the No. 47 this morning to see her. Apparently, he's a beautiful little thing, full head of black hair an' all!'

'Obviously not one of mine then.' George raised his hand thespian style to scratch his bald head.

'Waaaay!' More cheering.

'It's just a shame Tommy couldn't be here to see his little lad. Any news of Tommy's release date, George?'

'Yeah, I believe he's out on parole this week. Jack's already rearranged their wedding at St. Mary Magdalene's for midsummer's day.'

'Ah that's good. Jack's been a good dad to Tommy over the years.' To a man, the bar nodded approval; together, they toasted the news.

'What time you intend closing this afternoon, Ken?'

'Two o'clock, of course, Uncle. Jesus, what a question to ask your favourite landlord! Wouldn't want to break the law now, would I? Not on this holy day!'

'Good. Just make sure the door is locked tight and everyone is round the back in the snug. And for God's sake, knock that sodding racket on the head, will ya? You won't want any of my lot sniffing around once they pile out the Antigallican.'

The 'sodding racket' referred to was coming from a beat-up upright piano standing in the corner of the bar. Everyone pretty much agreed that it qualified as a musical instrument, but the din emanating from this contraption was unbelievable. The upright had survived two world wars without ever needing tuning - apparently... George, having gone to St. Olave's grammar school and taken violin lessons from a young age, knew without question that this piano was in dire need of tuning, and the sooner the better.

'Alright George, I'm ringing last orders in twenty minutes anyway, so I'm on it.'

'Good lad. Now...' whispered George behind the back of his hand '... chuck us a quick half of brown, will ya? I'm bloody parched.' A half-pint mug of brown was slid into George's waiting fist. After a quick look around the bar, seeing everybody was engaged with whatever tune was being cruelly beaten from the upright, George raised the mug to his lips, its contents magically disappearing long before anyone could claim witnesses to the event.

'K-ahhhh ... cheers Ken. On the house then? Nice touch, me ol' son, much appreciated. Be good now. Must get going. No peace for the wicked.'

'Right-Oh Uncle! Take it steady old 'n.'

George strolled out from the boozy smoke into the fresh air of a fine Sunday afternoon, the warm sun on his face, the melody of the barrel organ in his ears. Replacing his police helmet, he took hold of the handlebars of his bike, kicked the pedal with his left foot, and, with a push and a pump on the handlebars, he was mobile once more, his right leg hovering above the saddle until, after what seemed an age, he regained his balance, his right foot landing squarely on the other pedal and with the distant laughter from the pub fading into the distance, away wobbled Uncle George.

'Despite all we've had to deal with these last few years,' he mused. 'This ain't such a bad place is it?'

Chapter 3

Tower Bridge Magistrates Court and Police Station

Tower Bridge Magistrates Court was an imposing construction built from red brick and pale limestone. To the left of the magistrates court sat the police station, its blue lamp suspended over Tooley Street. The locale was dominated by Tower Bridge, which lurked in the background. Its iconic twin towers, grey-blue steel, and stonework punctured the London skyline. The surrounding streets bustled with red, double-decker buses and a constant stream of trucks and delivery vans carrying goods to and from the nearby docks and warehouses. The River Thames was a constant presence, with its distinctive smell, a mixture of saline water and industrial activity. There was an acrid tang in the air, mixed with the scent of coal smoke and diesel from passing ships. The distant sound of marine horns and engines echoed in the distance, blending with the rumble of the traffic.

Upon entering the police station your admiration of grandiose architecture and timeless heritage would swiftly end. From the dimly lit reception area, several corridors extended away into the distance to who knows where which clang and clatter with other-worldly activity echoing along the walls. The smell of highly polished floors permeated the underlying aroma of tea and sweat and the hint of a working canteen somewhere in the distance. Coupled with the sound of hobnailed boots and jangling keys you would want your visit to last no longer than necessary. The atmosphere along Tooley Street would be infinitely preferable with its mixed aroma of salty air, stinking mudflats, coal and diesel fumes.

Detective Sergeant Snell stood before Police Sergeant Alan Baines, thumbing through a ledger of charge sheets.

'When's this wrong'n getting out Desk?'

Sergeant Baines did not care for DS Snell's manner, nor did he care to be referred to as 'Desk'—what am I, your bloody personal assistant?

'Wrong'n Snell?'

'Yeah, you know who. Tommy bloody Baker.'

'I understand Tommy is out on parole tomorrow, Snell.'

'Tommy' now is it?'

'That's his name, Snell.'

DS Snell lifted his eyes from the charge sheets and glared at Sergeant Alan Baines.

'May I remind you, Desk, that I am a detective sergeant? I would appreciate some respect when you address me. Try Detective Sergeant.'

Baines raised his eyes from his paperwork. 'I'm not sure you outrank me, Snell. I suppose this why you call me Desk? How about from now on, you address me as Sergeant Baines?'

'I'm a Detective Sergeant Desk, not a fucking wooden top. I outrank a Desk Sergeant any day of the week. Got it?'

'No you fucking don't!' boomed a voice from behind a frosted glass window across the hall baring the name 'Detective Inspector R. Bellinger'.

'In here Snell, now!'

Snell tossed the charge sheets onto Baines' desk and, with a grimace, stormed into DI Bellinger's office. Snell dragged a chair across the parquet floor, plopped down, and crossed his arms.

Bellinger remained focused on his paperwork. 'Did I ask you to sit down Snell?'

'Err, no. No Sir you didn't.'

'No I don't believe I did. Anyway, now you've made yourself nice and comfortable, go and close the door, will you? There's a good chap.'

Snell hunched his shoulders, raising his hands at the snub. He rose noisily from his seat and grabbed the door handle.

'Don't slam it Snell, just close it.'

Snell silently closed the door and ambled back to his chair.

'Don't sit down. I've got a job for you, for which I would appreciate your immediate consideration'. Bellinger took his pen and, endorsing the page he was working on, closed the manila folder, rose from his chair and offered it to Snell, giving him a look. 'Take this back to your desk and give it a good going over, please. I've marked it urgent so there should be no confusion about when I want this done and dusted. Shall we say by the end of the week?'

'Yes, Sir'.

'Good. And one more thing, Snell - what's your beef with Baines? Did he upset you in a previous life or something?'

'I can't get on with him Sir; he's so bloody high-and-mighty the way he carries on. As if he was my guvnor or something. I'm a detective sergeant; I outrank him. He should show me more respect.'

'You can only command respect, Snell, not demand it. And I don't see much commanding going on right now.'

Snell's face hardened.

'And no, he doesn't outrank you. You are both sergeants and if I may remind you, you're both playing for the same fucking side, so why all the attitude?'

'It's personal Sir'.

'Go on'.

'I'd rather not say Sir'.

'Listen Snell, I don't care if he's your ex-boyfriend. Tell me what your problem is, unless you want me to conduct a disciplinary, at which point you'll be obliged to tell me AND everyone else who happens to be in the room'.

'He's big mates with Tommy Baker Sir, and I don't trust the pair of them.'

'Tommy who?'

Snell smiled. 'Tommy Baker Sir. I nicked him back in December. Put him Wandsworth for six.'

'How do you know they're mates?'

'They've known each other since junior school. They went to Fair Street together.'

'And this is a reason to disrespect a fellow police officer? Because he went to school twenty-odd years ago with a convicted criminal?'

'Don't suppose Sir.'

'What did you nick Tommy ... whatever his name is ... for?'

'Tommy Baker Sir. I nicked him for petty larceny.'

'Nicking stuff! Are fucking kidding me! Half the people living around here are on the scrounge somewhere. Jesus, if we collared every wanker stealing we'd be up to our arseholes in paperwork. What was so special about Tommy bloody Baker?'

'I'd rather not say Sir.'

'Snell! Just go back to your desk and get on with that folder in your hands. And try not to screw it into a complete ball.'

'Yes, Sir'.

Snell spun on his heels and headed towards the door. He paused.

'Sir?'

'Yes... Snell?'

'I was wondering how my transfer request is proceeding, Sir.'

'Your transfer request, Snell?'

'Yes, Sir, my request for a transfer to the Met?'

'Your request for a transfer to the Metropolitan Police Force? The cream-de-la-fucking-cream of all the entire London police forces?'

'Yes, Sir'.

'Do you really think the Met wants you, Snell? You can't even play nice with your own team mates. What makes you think you can cope with a rumble on a violent criminal?'

Snell dropped his head and stared at the floor. 'Sir, does this mean...'

'Snell, get out of my office. And ask Baines to pop in please'.

'Baines Sir? But he's not a detective ...'

'Just fucking do it, will you!'

'Yes, Sir'.

Snell stormed from Bellinger's office, banging the door shut as he exited and, with a grimace, gazed skyward, immediately remorseful of his behaviour. He strode by Baines' workstation. 'Bellinger wants to see you,' he mumbled.

Baines looked up in surprise. 'Me?'

Snell stopped in his tracks, glaring at Baines. 'Yes you, you prick'.

Baines put down his pen and called over to an officer standing front-0f-house. 'Constable Jordan, please be kind enough to man this desk for me for a moment. Inspector Bellinger wants to have a little chat.' Baines smiled at Snell as he clomped down the corridor.

'Certainly, Sarge,' complied Jordan.

A door slammed loudly down the passageway, echoing along the pale green walls.

Baines grinned. 'I guess Snell made it back to his office OK then?' Constable Jordan raised his eyebrows, smiled and shook his head. Baines crossed the hall and tapped on Bellinger's door.

'Come on in Baines.' Baines opened the door and stood at the entrance. 'Come in, take a seat, there's a good chap. There's something on my mind that I hope perhaps you can help me with.'

Sergeant Baines closed the door as gently as he could and took the seat offered him.

Chapter 4

Jonathan Albert Baker

Vine Lane Buildings was nestled near the banks of the River Thames, between Tooley Street and Mark Brown's Wharf. The aroma of coffee, grains, spices, and tea overpowered the distinct scent of the river, and a concoction of salty water mingled with the earthy smell of mudflats exposed at low tide. From the washing lines on the flat roof of Vine Lane Buildings, the Tower Bridge and the balletic progression of ships' funnels and masts against the skyline could be seen. The air was filled with shouted orders, the clanking of chains, and the steady thud of crates being moved. The walkways echoed with the voices of children playing hopscotch or chasing a ball around. Mothers chatted with neighbours, watching their little ones while exchanging gossip or sharing news about rationing and the latest fashions. The residents knew each other well and had a strong sense of community. People looked out for one another, sharing what little they had and supporting each other through difficult times. The area was close-knit, with a network of relationships built on shared experiences and mutual assistance.

Jonathan 'Jack' Albert Baker, a street bookmaker with a long list of loyal customers, stepped out of his flat into the bright April sunshine. Always dressed smartly in his double-breasted, grey pin-striped suit and crisp white shirt, Jack lived up to his nickname *'The Hollywood Docker'*. With his swept-back silver hair, blue eyes, and infectious smile, Jack's overall appearance and general demeanour commanded admiration from those with whom he engaged.

Jack's wife Harriet had taken the day off her cleaning jobs and had got the bus up to the Time and Talents in Bermondsey Street to meet her lady friends so Jack knew he had the day pretty much to himself until tea time. He walked the length of Vine Lane Buildings, nodding to familiar faces along the way until he reached the wall that separated the grounds from Mark Brown's Wharf. Turning the corner, checking there was nobody around to monitor his progress, Jack strolled around the back of the buildings where the communal wash house was situated. Fumbling for a key in his waistcoat pocket he unlocked the door to the room that held the copper washing boilers. Satisfied that nobody else was around, he locked the door behind him and headed back to the drying area. Here, an old cast iron fireplace was set into the brickwork, which had been out of use since the bombings during the 1940s smashed the structure of the chimney stack. Reaching up inside the flue Jack removed a brick that seemed not quite to fit the original coursework. Laying the brick on the floor, Jack produced a marble diary and a black and red cash box with a brass handle from deep within the brickwork. Checking once more, for sounds of anyone nearby, Jack unlocked and opened the red and black box. He counted out a sum of grubby, white, five-pound notes and carefully folded and slipped them into a leather bus conductor's cash satchel that he always wore beneath his Crombie overcoat. He relocked the red and black box, replaced it back in the flue along with the diary, and repositioned the wayward brick with care, being careful not to disturb the years of dirt and filth that caked the fireplace so as not to alert any enquiring eyes there had been any disturbance.

Exiting the wash house and locking the door behind him, Jack re-walked the length of Vine Lane Buildings until he reached Tooley Street, whereupon, turning right in the general direction of London Bridge, he crossed the road to Shand Street. Jack took another moment to look around and take in the scene. Satisfied there were no onlookers he walked along Shand Street until he reached the dimly lit cover of the tunnel under the railway lines from London Bridge Station amidst the familiar smell of the grain warehouses that populated the tunnel space. Peering into the tunnel's darkness, he checked his ex-army H. Samuel 'ACME LEVER' pocket watch and waited.

At 12.20 pm, a black Austin 12 saloon car pulled up at the entrance to Shand Street from the Crucifix Lane end. The driver stepped out of the vehicle, lit up a cigarette, took a good look around, got back into the driver's seat, and swung the car into the entrance to the tunnel. The headlamps flickered into life as the vehicle bounced over the wooden cobbles. The driver suddenly braked and stalled the car as a train from London Bridge Railway Station trundled and thundered above the tunnel roof, obliterating all other sounds.

'Jesus, what a fucking place,' muttered the driver. After several attempts, the driver restarted the car and continued his journey. As the car emerged from the gloom of the tunnel the driver's attention was drawn to a well-appointed, elderly gentleman attired in a pin-stripped grey suit beneath a knee-length Crombie overcoat standing at the junction of Hollyrood Street. The driver wound down the window.

'Jack Baker?' demanded the driver, his voice gruff and impatient.

'Who wants to know?' Jack replied, his eyes narrowing with suspicion.

'Are you Jack Baker, yes or no!' the driver barked, his fingers tapping the steering wheel.

'What do you want with Jack Baker, mister? Who are you anyway?' Jack countered, taking a step back from the car.

'Well, if you are Jack Baker, the Dennetts sent me to pick you up,' the driver said, his tone softening slightly.

Jack's jaw tightened. 'I'm not waiting for anyone called Dennett. I'm meeting a business associate.'

'Yeah, I know who you're waiting for. Your associate told me,' the driver said with a smirk.

'Who told you? Who told you what?' Jack demanded, his hand instinctively moving to the satchel inside his jacket.

'Your business associate,' the driver replied, emphasising the words mockingly. 'He told me.'

'Why isn't he here himself?' Jack asked, his eyes darting around the street.

'Ah, well he's had a bit of trouble at work. A bit of an accident, you might say,' the driver explained, his voice low. 'Here, get in the car. I'm here to take you to see the Dennetts.'

'Go fuck yourself,' Jack spat. 'I'm not going anywhere with you. Tell me what the hell's going on.'

The driver's patience was wearing thin. 'Jack, just get in the fucking car, please. I'm not here for conversation. I've got an errand to run, and you're it.'

Jack's eyes narrowed further. 'Are you the filth? You look like a bloody copper, driving a copper's car an' all.'

'I'm not a copper, Jack,' the driver insisted, exasperation creeping into his voice. 'I'm your driver for today. Now get in the car and stop fucking about.'

'Where're we going?' Jack asked, still hesitant.

'We're going back to Vine Lane Buildings, where you came from,' the driver replied matter-of-factly.

Jack's eyebrows shot up in surprise. 'How do you know I .....'

The driver cut him off, his voice laced with impatience. 'Jack, don't be silly. I can get there quicker without you on board, and you'll miss all the fun by the time you get back on foot.'

Jack scratched his head in frustration, momentarily exposing his leather bus conductor's satchel, suddenly mindful of the cash he was carrying. The driver appeared not to notice.

'I'm sitting in the back, right behind you, in case you start any funny business,' ordered Jack. 'I'm tooled up, so you better behave yourself.' Jack checked his pocket for the familiar feel of his door key.

'Alright, get in the back then. I don't give a fuck so long as I don't have to hang around this shit hole of a place any longer than I need to.'

The driver reached over his seat and pulled the leather strap releasing the catch on the rear door. Jack opened the door and peered inside; nothing but the smell of old leather and cigarettes. Jack climbed into the rear of the car and, upon taking his seat, took his heavy iron door key out of his pocket.

'Come on then,' demanded Jack pulling the rear door shut. 'Let's get on with it, and like I said no funny business.' Jack raised the key and jabbed it into the back of the driver's neck.

'What the fuck is that, Jack?'

'Like I said, I'm tooled up, so it's your choice. Be nice or be dead.'

'You haven't got the balls Jack.'

'Yeah? Well you never went to Ypres did you, you flash ponce. I've seen plenty of claret out there, ol' son, more than anyone would ever want to see again. This little beauty is an army issue, and I know how to use it. So don't think I won't. Now just drive the fucking car and, for God's sake, get on with it; your fucking aftershave's making me sick to my stomach.'

The driver, checking out the situation from the single rear-view mirror that Austin Motor Company offered its customers, could see none of Jack's deception, so he decided that getting Jack to his destination as fast as possible was better than the alternative Jack was offering.

'OK, Jack, sit back. I'm no hero and don't intend to prove otherwise.'

'Very wise,' smiled Jack. 'Now stop fucking about, and let's get on with it.'

Leaving Shand Street, the driver turned the car right onto Tooley Street and immediately left into Vine Lane. Passing Brewster's General Store and Ironmongery, the car pulled into the gates of the Vine Lane buildings.

'You can pull over here,' called out Jack.

'Jack I need to take you to the Dennetts. They're expecting you.'

'Don't care what you need. Stop the car and let me out here.'

'Jack I can't ...'

'Just do it you wanker! If you take me into the building's square, you'll start tongues wagging, and I'll be a marked man turning up in what they will think is a copper's car. Just stop here and let me out. If anyone sees me here, they'll assume I've been collared and let off with a caution.'

'Jack I ....'

Jack stabbed the iron key into the driver's neck once more. 'Listen you arsehole. You can drive out of here in this car or be driven out of here in a fucking ambulance. So if I were you I'd turn this car around, let me out and fuck off. You choose.'

The driver sighed and turned the car around to face the gates.

'Stop here, put the handbrake on, kill the engine and pass me the keys.'

'Take it easy Jack. Like I said I'm just the driver.' The driver handed Jack the keys over his shoulder. Jack stepped out of the car and threw the keys over the bonnet into the centre of the concourse.

'See those keys on the floor over there?'

'Yeah, so what?'

'Those keys need to stay there until you see me turn the corner into the grounds. If I see you leave the car before I turn the corner, you'll hear a loud bang, at which point you will hit the floor in a lot of pain. Do you understand?'

The driver nodded.

'So, say you understand.'

'Jack, I get it. Now, for God's sake, get lost, will yer?'

Jack turned on his heels and, walking backwards as quickly as he could, shuffled to the corner of Vine Lane Buildings, hiding the 'lethal' door key behind his back. With one final look around and deciding that the situation was in his favour, Jack Baker disappeared into the catacomb of passages and walkways of Vine Lane buildings. As he wound his way to a safe spot Jack heard the starter motor of an Austin fire up the engine and listened as the black saloon rumbled away back down Vine Lane and off into the distance.

Jack's heart thundered as he turned the key to his flat slamming the door behind him. Who the hell were the Dennetts and what did they want with him? He still had the stack of fivers in his satchel which he could not risk hiding in the two-roomed flat as there was no real place to hide it. And anyway, Harriet would no doubt find it, and if she knew he was packing so much cash, all hell would break loose. The options were limited. One would be to stay in the flat and lay low but take the risk that the Dennetts, whoever they were, would no doubt find him courtesy of the grapevine, at which point he would risk losing the cash. Another would be to stash the money back in the washhouse fireplace and take the consequences from whoever was interested in his business. At least the cash would be safe, even if he may not be.

Jack stepped out in the sunlight, locking the door behind him. He checked the square for strangers and decided the coast was clear. As he pondered his next move, an elderly woman burdened with a large sack of washing turned the corner. Louie Allen took on washing for others when their work commitments or their kids demanded their time. As Louie approached, she recognised Jack and called out.

'Alright, Jack! No work today, sweetheart?'

'No Louie, not today. But 'ere you shouldn't be lugging that bloody great sack around at your age. Here, give it here, I'm doing bugger all else anyway.'

'Aww Jack. That's so kind of you my lovely.'

'I know,' winked Jack, 'not many of us gentlemen left around here no more.'

'So bleeding true Jack.'

Jack took the bag of washing from Louie's arms and threw it over his shoulder, his legs buckling under the effort.

'Stone me, what you got in here, me love. Anvils?'

'Yeah, feels like it, don't it!' laughed Louie.

As the pair turned the corner to the communal wash house the hairs on Jack's neck stood on end. The door was ajar.

'Err ... Louie, you got any more washing to do today?'

'Yeah, Jack', said Louie. 'I got another bag to get, but nowhere near as big as this one.'

Jack thought for a moment, then, dropping the sack to the floor, turned to face Louie.

'Tell you what, Lou, I'll drop this one in, you nip back and get the other one, and I'll wait for you 'til you get back.' At least this would get Louie out of harms way if there was trouble ahead.

'Aww Jack, you sure?'

'Yeah, course I am. Go on, you get back, and I'll take care of things this end.'

Louie Allen marched off, waving to Jack and disappeared around the corner. Jack picked up the wash bag and, holding it before him, pushed the door open. The door swung open and crashed into the wall. The smell of wash salts and bicarbonate hit Jack's nose. Someone had been here recently doing some washing. One of the copper boilers was gurgling away while a pile of wet washing was dripping from the lines in the drying room. Everything appeared normal; it was just another washing day. Jack dumped the sack in the corner by the boilers, closed the main door and locked it. With haste, Jack knelt before the fireplace and reached up inside the flue, groping for the brick. Having located it and placing it on the floor beside him he noticed that the usual coating of dirt and grime had been disturbed.

'*That's fucking odd*,' thought Jack. He then reached up again for the cash box but the void was empty. Jack bounded back in disbelief. Once again, he checked the flue, this time not so cautiously, scrambling around the bricks inside the flue in case he got the wrong one.

Fuck me! Where's the fucking cash box? Panicking, Jack searched the drying room and the wash house for evidence of a red and black cash box but found none.

Gone!

Not knowing what to do next, Jack tried to gather his thoughts, but all he could hear was his pulse thumping loud and clear inside his head. Watch out, Jack! Hold fast! It then occurred to Jack that Louie was on her way back with another bag of washing so he had to get the situation back under control fast. He replaced the brick and swept back the disturbed soot and dirt with the wash house yard brush. Slapping the dirt and grime from his trousers Jack checked his hair, straightened the seams of his suit trousers, unlocked the wash house door and stepped out into the sunlight.

Before him stood two strangers, one holding a marbled diary and the other a black and red cash box with a brass handle.

'Hello Jack, how have you been?' The man's voice was smooth as silk, but an underlying edge set Jack's teeth on edge.

'And you are?' asked Jack, his eyes narrowing as he studied the two strangers before him.

'Me, Jack? My name is Liam Dennett and you, if I'm correct, are Jack Baker.' The man's lips curled into a smile that didn't reach his eyes.

'What can I do for you?' Jack's tone was cautious, his hand instinctively moving to his satchel.

'Well, Jack, for a start, you can tell me why you and your associate were so keen to place a bet with us at The Woodstock Junction Horse Trot meeting at Kingston next Monday?' Liam's voice dripped with false friendliness.

'Were we?' Jack feigned ignorance, his mind racing to figure out how much these men knew.

'Yes Jack, you were. And what's more, your associate was keen not to let us know that you'd managed to pay off one of the teams to throw the race between the pair of you. Might even be a bit of horse doping involved as well.' Liam's eyes glittered dangerously.

'He told you all that? That's not like any associate of mine,' smiled Jack, trying to maintain his composure. 'They wouldn't be so fucking stupid.'

'Oh, he didn't want to tell us at first, but, like you, Jack, we have very persuasive ways of getting the facts if required. A bit like the way you persuaded our driver.' Liam's smile widened, revealing teeth that seemed way too large.

The smile left Jack's face, a cold dread settling in his stomach. 'What have you done to Harry? Where is he? He was supposed to meet me earlier.'

'Unfortunately, Jack, your obnoxious little friend, has cancelled all appointments for today and is unavailable for comment as he is unconscious.' Liam's casual tone belied the threat in his words.

Jack tried to swallow but his throat had dried, his heart pounding. 'What have you done with Harry? He wouldn't hurt a fly. He's in his late 60s, for God's sake.'

'Harry will be fine, I'm sure. Nedser can be a bit of a brute when he doesn't get his own way, but Harry was extremely cooperative. Didn't take too much persuasion, did it Neds?' Liam glanced at his companion.

Nedser laughed. 'He was very informative. Even cried like a baby in the end. Must have been all that tension leaving him once he owned up.'

Liam continued his voice hardening. 'So as we see it, you pair of slags had rigged a trotting race to bet a large sum against the book - our book.'

'What d'you mean, your book?' Jack's fingers twitched, itching to protect his money satchel.

'We run the streets now Jack, from Dockhead and Jamaica Road up to Tooley Street.' Liam's voice was filled with smug satisfaction.

'I run Tooley Street, pal, not you,' Jack growled, his blue eyes flashing angrily.

'Ah, this is why we wanted to talk to you earlier, but you weren't keen to cooperate. Maybe you are now?' Liam's tone was light, but the threat was clear.

'You reckon?' Jack's voice was low, dangerous.

'Yes Jack, we do. Today, old son, is your last day conducting business on Tooley Street. Either you hand over your book and walk away, or you will be carried away.' Liam's words hung like a death sentence, the tension between the men thick enough to cut with a knife.

Jack grabbed the lapel of his waistcoat and pointed to his war medal. 'You see this? This is for bravery in the face of the enemy. You don't get these by listening to Irish cunts like you!' Jack lunged forward and, with speed, punched a left and right fist into Liam's face, knocking him to the ground. The marbled diary span from Liam's hand and slid to Nedser's feet.

Liam rose to his feet wiping his bleeding lip. 'That wasn't very nice, Jack. Could have ended badly.'

'Not bad enough, you pikey bastard.'

Liam raised his fists boxer style, circling around Jack as a cat might entrap a vole. 'Now we let the games begin.'

As Liam prepared to charge a crashing head blow from behind felled Jack like a rag doll. The last thing Jack recalled was to feel the boots driving into him as he lost consciousness.

Louie Allen lifted the sack of washing from behind her neighbour's dustbin and headed off to the communal wash house. From within a kitchen along her walk she could smell a dinner being cooked as the steam from the stove billowed out from the open kitchen window. Louie could hear *Oh, Oh Antonio* coming from the Light Programme. 'Wow', she thought, 'that Florrie Forde couldn't half belt it out! She walked the length of Vine Lane Buildings singing her heart out, *Oh, Oh Antonio, He's Gorn Awaaaay ...*' smiling all the while until she reached Mark Brown's Wharf; after that, she turned the corner and froze, dropping the washing sack with a thump. There, lying face down on the ground outside the door of the communal wash house, lay Jack Baker in a pool of blood. Beside his still body lay an empty leather bus conductor's cash satchel. Two men, crouched by Jack's side searching his pockets, stood bolt upright when they heard the thump of the wash sack. Louie raised her hands to her head and, for all she was worth, cried out in anguish.

The two stared at each other until, with a flick of Liam's head, Nedser turned and strode towards Louie.

'Leave it!' called Liam, pointing upwards. Windows were opening above them, and several heads were poking out, gasping in horror at what they were witnessing.

The Dennetts ran for it.

Chapter 5

Tower Bridge Police Station

'Sergeant Baines, I want you to help me with something.'

Baines looked quizzically at Bellinger. 'Me Sir? What can I do to help you? Don't you have your own boots on the ground?'

'Yes, Sergeant, I do, but I want to keep this one out of the limelight. In particular I don't want Snell anywhere near this. He'll just fuck it up again. Please arrange for two of your men to pick up Tommy Baker from Wandsworth nick tomorrow at 13.00 hours. There'll be a car assigned to them for the day. This is sensitive. Am I clear?'

'Yeah, crystal, Sir. Is there anything you can share with me? Why Tommy Baker? He's hardly Dick Turpin. He was done for petty larceny not a gold bullion job.'

'Yes there is something I can share with you. Tommy's dad, Jack Baker, you know him?'

'Yes, Sir, I've known him since my school days with Tommy. I believe he's a street bookie now. It's not uncommon around here. Nothing too serious to warrant constant vigilance. Bit of a war hero if I recall.'

'That's the bloke, alright. Constable George Turner brought this latest incident to my attention. Jack was given a bloody good kicking two days ago, and he's currently in intensive care at Guy's Hospital. An eye witness who matched their descriptions to photos we received from The Home Office. It looks like the Dennett brothers gave him a good going over.'

'Bastards!'

'Bastards indeed. And the very same bastards we've been wanting to collar for a long time.'

'So why haven't we?'

'Not our call I'm afraid. The Dennetts are under surveillance from the Counter Terrorism Branch, Security Service. MI5 are after the big fish not these scumbags. The Dennett brothers are too far down the food chain. Apparently, if we step in now, we'll scare the big fish away. Then the big fish go into hiding for a while, and it all starts over again with another bunch of lowlife morons doing the footwork.'

'So why are we giving Tommy Baker a lift home?'

'You're not giving him a lift home. You are to bring him here to me. He doesn't know yet that his dad's been beaten up. Warden Rossi doesn't allow visitors in the last week before a release. Apparently, it gets them all jittery, so nobody will have been to see Tommy to give him the bad news. Probably a good job. I reckon if he knew he'd tear the place up and ruin his parole.'

'So you want to tell him yourself, is that it?'

'Sort of, but it's more than that. I can't let this near Snell. He'll have a field day with it. I need Tommy as bait to lure the Dennett brothers. He'll go after them once he finds out what they did to his dad. I want him to go after them but with our support. The Dennetts will be expecting him, but they won't expect us. They're bound to be packing, so if we can get them in mid-flow, we'll nail the fuckers on our own terms and bring them in. Got it?'

'Got it Sir. Are we involved or is it just CID?'

'Everybody if needs be. We'll work out the details later. We first need to get Tommy back and safe, maybe keep him here for a while until he calms down. Without him we'll have no reason to get involved with the Dennetts. I believe he'll be cooperative until he gets the news, at which point I also believe the shit will hit the fan, which is why I need two of your best men.'

'OK Sir, I get it.'

'Good. Now, who do you trust? Who will you send for Tommy who won't go shouting their mouth off?'

'Well, there's Constable Jordan; he's on the desk now.'

'Yeah, Jordan, he'll do. Who else?'

'For this job? There's only one other person I'd trust with this. George Turner.'

'Ah yeah. Uncle George! Good shout, Sergeant. Where is he right now?'

'Right now I reckon he's getting ready to finish his beat and head back to the station.'

"Good, have him come and see me the moment he clocks off.'

'It's done Sir. But what about Snell? Won't he get wind of it?'

'Don't you worry about Snell. He's destined for greater things. I've just signed off his transfer to the Met!'

Baines' face lit up. 'Fuck me! Do they know what they're letting themselves in for!'

'Who cares? They might be the finest police unit in the whole of London, but they're fucking shit at character assessment!'

Out on the desk, Constable Jordan paused from his ledger and peered at the frosted glass of DI Bellinger's office. He was sure he could hear laughter.

Chapter 6

Ignazio Rossi

Prison officer Williams unlocked the door to Tommy's cell and, folding his arms, leaned against the door frame with a weary sigh. His eyes scanned the small, dingy space before settling on Tommy.

'Tommy.'

'Yeah,' came the curt reply from the young man seated on the narrow bunk.

'Warden wants a chat,' Williams said, his tone neutral but tinged with a hint of urgency.

Tommy sat up, suspicion etched across his face. 'What about?'

Williams shrugged, his uniform creasing with the movement. 'Why would he tell me? He wants a word before you go. Standard procedure, I reckon.'

'Not interested. Sorry, I'm going home,' Tommy retorted, his jaw set stubbornly.

'Tommy, you need to talk to Rossi,' Williams pressed, a note of exasperation creeping into his voice.

Tommy's eyes flashed with anger. 'Fuck Rossi, what's he want with me? I'm out of here.'

'Tommy....' Williams began but was cut off.

'What does he want?' Tommy demanded, his hands grabbing the edge of the bunk.

'Better ask him?' Williams suggested, raising an eyebrow.

'Fuck this, I'm out,' Tommy growled, standing to confront the officer.

'Tommy....' Williams said again, this time more forcefully.

'What?' Tommy snapped.

'This might be a good idea?' Williams offered, his tone softening.

'Why?' Tommy asked, curiosity finally overcoming his defiance.

'C'mon son, it's alright. Just a chat, nothing more,' Williams coaxed, his face showing a hint of sympathy.

Tommy hesitated, then asked warily, 'Am I gonna be arrested on my way out?'

'I doubt it. It happens sometimes - but not today. Anyway, that's not what this is about and I know it's not what Rossi wants to talk to you about. So come on, you daft bugger, follow me. And for God's sake sit on your fucking hands when you're in his office. This is your chance, kiddo,' Williams explained, his voice a mix of exasperation and encouragement.

'I don't understand...' Tommy mumbled, confusion evident in his furrowed brow.

'You will. Trust me,' Williams assured him, gesturing for Tommy to follow.

'Trust you?' Tommy repeated, scepticism clear in his voice.

'Yeah. Trust me, and believe it,' Williams insisted, his eyes meeting Tommy's with a look of sincerity that finally seemed to break through the young man's resistance.

'Please, sit yourself down, Tommy'.

Ignazio Rossi cut an impressive figure, with the bearing of an individual who'd overcome numerous hurdles and emerged victorious. He sat at his desk while Tommy took his place opposite. On either side of Tommy stood two prison officers, McEwan and Williams, both exceptionally good at their jobs.

Rossi, seemingly content with form filling, dipped his pen into the ink pot, shaking the spill onto the blotter. He raised his head and looked around the room, first at Tommy, then at McEwan and Williams.

'Err.. gentlemen, will you excuse us, please?'

With hands clasped before them as if in prayer, McEwan and Williams stared at each other with raised eyebrows.

'Sir?' asked McEwan.

'Gentlemen, I would like you to leave the room, please'.

'But Sir...'

Rossi raised his eyes from his paperwork and offered a glance that convinced both officers this was not the time to say another word.

'Thank you, gentlemen; attend to your duties, please.'

'Sir, yes, Sir.'

As the echoes of footsteps diminished down the corridor, Rossi set aside his pen. He reclined in his seat, interlocking his fingers behind his head, and fixed his stare on Tommy. He remained silent. Tommy looked around the room, back at Rossi, and finally lowered his eyes to his feet and shuffled in his seat.

'So, Tommy,' said Rossi, breaking the silence. 'You're out today.'

'Yes, Warden, I hope so. I really hope so,' Tommy replied, a glimmer of anticipation in his eyes.

'Have you enjoyed your stay here Tommy?' Rossi's tone was deceptively casual.

Tommy looked up and glared at Rossi. 'Are you fucking kidding me?'

'Now, now, Tommy, no need for cursing,' Rossi chided. 'I'm asking you a simple question and expect a civil answer. Have you enjoyed your stay?'

Tommy swallowed hard, trying to rein in his frustration. 'It was no holiday, Guvner,' he muttered.

'Then maybe it's a holiday you need then, Tommy,' Rossi mused, a cryptic smile on his lips.

Confusion flickered across Tommy's face. 'I'm not with you, Guv, sorry?'

'That's OK, Tommy. I'm just saying. When was the last time you had a holiday? I mean, you know, seaside fun, wife and kids, all that stuff?' Rossi's eyes bore into Tommy, searching.

Tommy shifted uncomfortably in his seat. 'I don't have a wife; I only have a girlfriend and a baby right now. A baby I haven't seen yet,' he said, a note of pain in his voice.

'I understand. That can't be nice,' Rossi replied, his sympathy feeling hollow.

Frustration bubbled up in Tommy's chest. 'Guv, I need to leave here and go see my litt'n. I don't even know how Lizzie is. What's the point of this Guv? Why aren't I walking out of here already?'

Rossi slid the leather chair from underneath him with a soft creak and, raising his hand, beckoned Tommy. 'Come on, you. We have business to attend to. There's something I want you to do for me,' he said, his tone suddenly businesslike.

Tommy's brow furrowed with suspicion. 'Where are we going?'

'Just follow me,' Rossi commanded, already striding towards the door, 'before we lose you to the street again.' The implied threat hung between them as Tommy reluctantly rose to follow.

Rossi opened his office door and beckoned Tommy to follow. The pair walked out of the administration square and across the entrance court past the chapel. Adjacent to the chapel entrance, Rossi unlocked a door that led to a flight of steps, at which point he invited Tommy to enter.

'Go on in, Tommy, you first. Keep going up until you reach the balcony. See it up there?'

Tommy peered into the darkened staircase. 'Yeah I see it alright. Why am I going all the way up there? Remind me?'

'Because we have something we want to show you Tommy,' echoed a voice from above. Tommy looked up again to see a man of small stature leaning on the balcony, legs crossed, smiling.

'I'm gonna get a kicking ain't I,' shouted Tommy.

'Do I look like I'm the sort of bloke that enjoys giving young offenders a kicking, Tommy? Look at me, I'm in a suit, for God's sake, and it's just come out of the cleaners. Now get your arse up here before I change my mind.'

Tommy looked back at Rossi. Rossi smiled. 'Go on, Tommy, it's all OK. Commander Brem-Wilson is from the Home Office. They don't beat people up. That's our job!'

In anticipation of a rumble Tommy sprinted up the staircase to the balcony. When he got there he found himself staring down the barrel of a handgun. 'Enfield 80/200, in case you were wondering, Tommy. Just a precaution I can assure you. Warden Rossi, would you please join us?'

'Coming right up, chief,' Rossi called out as he bounded the steps, taking them two at a time. After ascending the stairs, Rossi fumbled for a keyring and chose a well-worn key to unlock the entrance to a stark room containing only a solitary table and four seats. 'This was a private interrogation room a long time ago, Tommy. We don't use it anymore; we're not allowed to. The Victorians used to love it though, you know, out of the way kind of place, away from prying eyes and all that.'

'So why am I here?' asked Tommy, his eyes darting nervously around the stark room.

Rossi spoke, his voice echoing slightly in the bare space. 'You're here, Tommy, because we want to show you some pictures we've taken. Kinda off the record sort of stuff. Isn't that right Commander?' He glanced over at Brem-Wilson, a hint of uncertainty in his tone.

Brem-Wilson strode purposefully across the room, his shoes clicking against the cold concrete floor. He approached the table that dominated the centre of the chamber. 'So, sit yourself down Tommy and take a good, long look at these,' Brem-Wilson instructed, his voice carrying an air of authority. He unlatched a leather valise, its surface cracked and scuffed from years of use. He extracted a stack of large format photographs from within, spreading them out methodically on the table before Tommy. The glossy black and white images gleamed under the harsh overhead light. 'You see these men, Tommy? Take your time now. Do you recognise any of them?' Brem-Wilson's eyes bored into Tommy, searching for any flicker of recognition.

Tommy leaned forward, his brow furrowed in concentration as he examined the photographs. Two men featured prominently in most of the images, their faces captured with startling clarity. Each picture depicted a different location - a bustling street corner, a dimly lit pub and a nondescript warehouse. Tommy's eyes darted from one image to the next, a bead of sweat forming on his upper lip as the weight of the situation pressed down upon him.

'Nah. Never seen these blokes before.'

'Tommy, I want you to consider your next answer very carefully. I'm going to ask you nicely one more time. Sadly there won't be a third. Do you recognise either of these two men?'

'I told you already. I ain't never seen them two before, and that's the God's honest truth.'

Brem-Wilson looked up at Rossi with raised eyebrows. 'What d'you reckon, Warden. Is he telling the truth?'

Rossi put his hand on Tommy's shoulder. 'Are you Tommy?'

'I swear, Guv, I've never laid eyes on 'em.'

Rossi and Brem-Wilson glanced at each other. Rossi nodded and shrugged his shoulders. Brem-Wilson looked back at Tommy, pulled a leather wallet from his inside jacket pocket, and slid it over to Tommy.

'Take a look inside, Tommy. It won't bite I can assure you.'

Tommy took the wallet and opened the clasp. Inside was Brem-Wilson's Home Office ID:

Commander Phillip Brem-Wilson
Counter Terrorism Branch
Security Service (MI5)

Tommy stared back at Brem-Wilson then at Rossi. 'What's all this got to do with me Guv? I ain't no terrorist. I was banged up for thieving food from the docks. I ain't no spy. I just wanna go home. I wanna see Lizzie and my baby. I haven't seen my baby yet. I wanna go home.'

Seeing Tommy was getting upset, Brem-Wilson took Tommy by the arm. 'Tommy, I think it's time we told you. But we had to be sure you're not an associate of these two. These gentlemen go by the names of Liam and Nedser Dennett. The Dennett family are from Enniskillen in County Fermanagh and were responsible for organising and deploying IRA attack raids on British army barracks in both Northern Ireland and the South of England. The purpose of the attacks was to acquire ordinance – guns, ammunition, explosives and other armaments. They're gun runners and IRA fundraisers, Tommy. We at the Secret Service want to put them away. And we believe you might be able to help us.'

Rossi cleared his throat and spoke in a firm but not unkind tone. 'So it's nearly noon, Tommy. Let's get you ready for release. Don't forget you're on parole, so behave yourself and listen to your head, not your gut. You won't want to be back in here ever again, not now you've got a family waiting for you. C'mon, let's get the paperwork done, and you can be on your way. I'm sure you're eager to get some fresh air and see your loved ones.'

Tommy furrowed his brow, confusion evident in his eyes. 'I don't get it, Guv. I just don't. What's all this got to do with me? Why are you telling me about these Dennett blokes?'

Rossi's expression remained neutral, but there was a hint of something unreadable in his gaze. 'You'll find out soon enough, Tommy. Soon enough. Just keep your wits about you when you're out there. The world's not always what it seems, especially for a man fresh out of prison.'

Chapter 7

They Called for Uncle

'You want me to do what?'

Constable George Turner gawped at Detective Inspector Bellinger as if he had just asked for his hand in marriage. His jaw hung slack, eyes wide with disbelief. 'You want me to go and fetch Tommy Baker from Wandsworth and bring him here? Are you serious, Sir?'

'That's exactly what I want you to do, George. I want you and Constable Jordan to take a marked police car from the pool and be outside Wandsworth nick when the gates open at 13.00 hours sharp. Warden Rossi will have primed Tommy that you'll be waiting for him, so there should be no surprises. I want the two of you there in case he kicks off or tries anything funny.'

'I get that, Sir, but why in blazes would we...'

'Constable, are you disobeying a senior officer's direct order?' Bellinger's tone sharpened, his eyes narrowing.

'No, Sir. Sorry, Sir, and all that, but none of this don't sound right to me. It's all a bit dodgy if you ask me.'

'Don't worry, it will make sense soon enough, but I can't explain it all now. Time is of the essence. Take Jordan, go get Tommy, and bring him here to me. And, he is to be treated nice, understood? No rough stuff.'

'Got it, Sir. Treat him with kid gloves, right.'

'Now get going. The Chief has signed off a car for you. No need for bells and whistles, I don't want any fuss. Just go get him and bring him here quietly. Oh, and George...'

'Yes, Sir?'

'He doesn't know his dad's in hospital, and he's not to know until I see him, understood? Not a peep about it.'

'Bugger me, I don't want to be a fly on the wall when that hits the fan. It'll be like lighting a powder keg.'

'Now d'you get it?'

'Yes Sir, I get it.'

'Alright, now go and grab Jordan and report to Sergeant Baines. He has the car keys and some paperwork for you to sign.'

Chapter 8

At the Gates of HMP Wandsworth

They say once you're outside the gates of HMP Wandsworth the first thing that hits you is the sweetness of the air. It doesn't matter how short your stay was. You never forget the smell inside Wandsworth. If you were lucky enough to have your own cell, the dimensions were so restrictive you could just about touch both opposing walls from a standing position. You had your own toilet and sink but rarely any hot water and if you were lucky, the toilet bowl wasn't cracked or broken. The only saving grace was that time spent at HMP Wandsworth was not long-term. Most of the inmates were only there for a while. The rats, however, never leave the place, and ironically, neither do the screws.

The first thing that caught Tommy's eye as he walked through the gatehouse was how green and lush the trees were in the park opposite Heathfield Road. In December, when he went in, there was nothing but bare branches and slushy streets. The second thing that caught his eye was a black police car with two officers eyeballing him.

'OK, here we fucking go again,' thought Tommy. 'A nice welcome committee I'm sure.' Tommy tucked his string-wrapped paper parcel under his arm and walked towards the road, at which point the police car doors opened, and both officers stepped out, putting on their helmets.

'Tommy!' called one of the officers.

Tommy tried not to look. 'I'm busy, mate; got a bus to catch.'

'Tommy, come over here you tosser!' insisted one of the officers.

Tommy jerked his head towards the pair. 'What do you two want? I ain't done nothing, I've been in there for four sodding months. I'm going home.'

'Tommy, come here, lad. I want a word with you. We've come to take you home.'

Tommy stopped in his tracks and took a long look at the pair. 'Is that you, George?' asked Tommy, squinting.

'Yes, Tommy. Now get in the car, please. Don't be a prat.'

Tommy sat in the back of the police car with his paper-wrapped parcel on his knees. George sat beside him while Jordan drove up front. The car sped through Clapham Common and along Clapham Road, heading towards The Elephant and Castle. From there, it went down the New Kent Road and along Tower Bridge Road. As the car approached the junction at Tooley Street, Jordan indicated right.

'That's the wrong way, mate,' declared Tommy, his voice tinged with frustration. 'I live at Vine Lane Buildings. You want a left here, not a right.'

'All in good time, Tommy,' George replied calmly. 'There's somebody wants a word with you at the station. We're popping in there first, just a quick detour.'

'You've gotta be fucking joking!' Tommy exploded, his face reddening. 'I need to get home and go see Lizzie and my kid. I haven't set eyes on him yet. Christ, I've been locked up for months!'

'Lizzie's fine, Tommy,' offered George, trying to soothe Tommy's agitation. 'Joyce from the pub went to see her over Easter. Your boy is fit and healthy, and Lizzie's made good her recovery. Now, for Gawd's sake, listen to me. We're taking you to see Detective Inspector Bellinger. He wants a word, that's all.'

'No way!' Tommy shook his head vehemently. 'Is that ponce Snell involved in this? I bet this is all his doing. He's had it in for me from the start.'

'No, Tommy,' confided George, his voice low and reassuring. 'Snell's got nothing to do with this. I promise you that.'

'That's bollocks,' Tommy spat, unconvinced. 'Snell wants me back in, I know it. He wants me to violate my parole and get banged up for the full term. I ain't having it, George. I ain't having none of it. You can't do this to me, not now!'

As the car pulled into Tower Bridge Police Station yard, Constable Jordan spoke for the first time.

'Tommy, I need you to calm down, please. You're not being nicked and you're not being held. What you are being asked to do is spend an hour with Detective Inspector Bellinger. He has some news you need to hear and some advice to give. Believe me, Tommy, the last thing you want to do right now is to cause a fuss in there. Everyone's on alert, and they're all a bit on edge right now. So please, no fuss and bother. George and I were specifically chosen for this little taxi run. Bellinger didn't want anyone else from the force involved. You OK with that?'

Tommy slumped back into the seat. 'I suppose so, but what's it all about?'

'Bellinger has all the details, Tommy,' assured George. 'Come on, he's waiting for you in his office.'

'Come on in, Tommy, take a seat, please.' Bellinger gestured towards the chair in front of him. 'Please accept my apologies for asking you here at such short and unexpected notice.'

'What's this about?' asked Tommy. 'You nicking me again for something I didn't do?'

'No, Tommy, you're not being nicked; you're here because we need your assistance in a police matter.'

'You gotta be kidding me. Why would I want to help the filth.'

George Turner flinched. 'Watch your mouth, Tommy, you're not in Wandsworth now. Please don't use that kind of language here; we don't appreciate it.'

Tommy turned to face up to George, saw the look on Jordan's face and thought better of it. Bellinger took control once again.

'Thank you, Constable Turner. Tommy, please sit down now. I will not let this interview get out of hand. Trust me.'

'Here we go again,' laughed Tommy. 'Why does every copper and screw want me to trust them after they've banged me up?'

'I'll explain. I personally requested that Constables Turner and Jordan pick you up from Wandsworth for two reasons. The first reason is that I can trust these two to keep their bloody mouths shut. Isn't that right gentlemen?' George and Jordan nodded. 'The second reason is that I have some grave news for you.'

Tommy snapped to attention. 'It's Lizzie right?'

'No Tommy it's not Lizzie, it's your dad'.

Tommy's face froze. He grabbed the arms of the chair and tensed up rising to his feet. Both constables were ready for him, so they grabbed his shoulders and forced him back into the chair. 'Ah fuck me don't tell you've nicked my dad. This is Snell again, yeah?'

'No Tommy,' replied Bellinger. 'He's not been nicked; he's been badly beaten up.'

This time, Tommy lunged forward towards Bellinger beyond the reach of the constables, fists on Bellinger's desk. 'You bastards, have you done him in? What has he ever done to piss you lot off? He's only...'

Jordan grabbed Tommy by his arm and wrenched it up the middle of his back, causing Tommy to yelp in pain. Bellinger stepped in. 'Sit down, Tommy, and get that anger out of your system. George, you go outside, and if anyone wants to know what the row's all about, you tell them we've got it under control here. Jordan, you stay here with me for a while. You don't know Constable Jordan, do you, Tommy.'

'I guess not, should I?'

'Not directly but Constable Jordan comes to us on loan from Special Branch. His 'speciality' is dealing with violent criminals. Isn't that right, Constable Jordan?'

'All true, Sir,' smiled Jordan, looking down at Tommy.

'Now, Tommy,' pleaded Bellinger, 'we can do this in one of two ways. We can do this nicely, or we can do it Constable Jordan's way. What d'you reckon, nice sounds better?'

'Nice sounds better,' agreed Tommy.

'Okey-dokey then. Constable, would you mind leaving us for a moment. Just wait outside with George for me, please. I'll handle this from here,' Bellinger said, his tone softening as he addressed Jordan. He could sense the tension in the room dissipating.

'You sure Sir?' Jordan asked, his hand hovering near the doorknob, a hint of concern in his voice.

'Yes Jordan, I can tell Tommy's worked it out. We didn't beat your dad up, Tommy, but we know who did, and I want you to help us nail the bastards. Deal?' Bellinger leaned forward, his eyes fixed on Tommy's face, searching for any sign of hesitation.

Tommy paused for a moment, weighing his options. He knew he was in a tight spot, but something about Bellinger's demeanour made him want to trust the man. 'Deal,' he agreed, his voice barely above a whisper.

'Right then,' said Bellinger, a hint of satisfaction in his voice. He turned back to Jordan, who was lingering by the door. 'Constable, I tell you what. While you're out there, can you rustle up four mugs of tea and bring them in here, please. Make sure they're good and strong – we've got a lot to discuss.'

Jordan nodded. 'Consider it done Sir,' he replied. Jordan left Bellinger's office and gently closed the door behind him. Tommy heard his footsteps echoing down the hall after a brief, muffled conversation with George.

'OK, here we go,' said Bellinger, leaning forward in his chair. 'Here's what happened. Do you know the Dennett brothers?'

Tommy furrowed his brow, trying to recall. 'The Dennett brothers? I've heard of them but I don't know them personally. What about them?'

'What do you know about them?' Bellinger pressed, his eyes fixed on Tommy's face.

Tommy shrugged, his frustration evident. 'I didn't know anything about them until this morning. Some geezer from the Security Service cornered me, telling me he needed my help. They're gun-runners or something to do with the IRA, apparently. Apart from that I ain't got a clue. Nor do I care, to be honest.'

Bellinger nodded, his expression grave. 'Well, we have an eye witness who is prepared to testify in front of a judge and jury that it was Liam and Nedser Dennett who took your dad out of action. We're not entirely sure why, but it all happened at the back of the washhouse at Vine Lane Buildings. The Dennetts run a book up by Dockhead on the Dickens Estate. We suspect they thought someone had bet against them and rigged a race in their favour. The Dennetts wouldn't have liked that one bit. They want all the juice to fund their friends over in Ireland, so if they'd lost a nice packet of cash courtesy of foul play, the big fish would not have been happy. One of the ladies who use the washhouse bumped into the Dennetts, but they scarpered once they saw her. Looking at his wounds, it appears one of them may have whacked your dad from behind, then the two of them probably took turns beating on him while he was defenceless on the floor.'

Tommy's face paled, his hands clenching into fists. 'Where is Dad now?' he asked, his voice barely above a whisper.

Bellinger's expression softened slightly. 'He's at Guy's Hospital, in the Intensive Care Unit. The doctors are doing everything they can for him.'

Tommy flinched baring his teeth. 'I'll fucking kill 'em!'

'Not so fast,' commanded Bellinger. 'We're going to help you get your own back, but, like I said, you must trust us.'

'Why should I trust you? It was your mongrel Snell that banged me up. And all for what, nicking a couple of boxes of tinned stuff from New Fresh Wharf? Bloody hell, everybody on the docks does that, so why pick on me?'

'Tommy, do you know why I specifically requested George and Jordan to help? Why I didn't use my own men?'

'Can't say I do.'

'It's because of Snell. I didn't want him involved. If Snell got wind of this and knows you're here with me the whole operation I have in mind to nail those Irish bastards will go pear-shaped. He'll turn the whole thing into his personal vendetta against you.'

'Well he's gonna find out soon enough anyway. He's your Sergeant ain't he?'

Bellinger smiled. 'Funny you should say that, Tommy. Actually... he's not anymore. I've signed off his transfer to another force. At this moment, he's probably having his induction training with the Met. So Tommy, from this moment onwards, Snell is no longer your, nor my, fucking problem.'

A rap on the glass pane announced the arrival of tea.

'Yep, come in, Jordan. Bring George with you please. Let's all sit down over here.' The four moved over to Bellinger's meeting table and took a seat.

'Now, Tommy, drink your tea. I'm out of here in five minutes. I have a meeting with the Chief Inspector. He wants me write a report about all this. All about you Tommy! Fame at last eh! How does that make you feel?'

'Not sure, Guv, only ever seen one police report, and that ended me up in Wandsworth.'

'Ah, OK, yeah, I get that,' continued Bellinger. 'But after you've drunk your tea Constables Turner and Jordan will accompany you on your forward journey.'

'Where we going?' asked Tommy.

'Guy's Hospital you soppy bastard! You're getting a VIP, chauffeur-driven ride to see Lizzie and baby James.'

Tommy slapped his hand to his face, unable to restrain his emotions.

'C'mon Billy-big-bollocks, drink up, let's go and see your baby,' offered George, ruffling Tommy's hair. 'And ... I'm told ... he's got a full Barnet of black hair just like you!'

Chapter 9

Tea and Ice Cream

A gentle breeze rustled through the budding leaves of the London plane trees that dominated Potters Fields Park. The sun cast a warm glow over everything, making it a perfect day to be outdoors. The paths were lined with blooming daffodils and tulips, adding yellow, red, and pink splashes to the landscape. A few families sat across the grassy area, spread out on picnic blankets. Mothers and fathers sat with their children, unpacking their simple lunches wrapped in wax paper: sandwiches, hard-boiled eggs, and apples all shared among the family members, while flasks of tea were poured into enamel mugs. The children's playground was a hive of activity, filled with laughter and the screams of youthful energy. The young ones took turns on the swings, flying high into the air with joyous abandon, while others raced each other down the metal slides, landing with a thump and a triumphant grin. Another group of children crowded around a merry-go-round, pushing it faster and faster as their excited squeals filled the air. Nearby, pairs of children laughed out loud as they balanced each other on see-saws, enjoying the simple thrill of the rise and fall.

On the wooden seat beneath the trees sheltering Antonio's ice cream trolley reclined Lizzie, James in her arms. She smiled as she watched the squabbling pigeons pilfering the broken ice cream cornets that spilled from Antonio's trolley. Around her were the ladies of Weaver's Lane. The spring weather had remained kind since the Easter weekend offering Lizzie plenty of opportunity to take the air and promenade James in his black, ironclad Royale pram.

From the door of the St. John's Tavern, Ken, the landlord, appeared carrying a tray piled high with tea cups and saucers. Joyce followed with a huge pot of sugared, milky tea.

"Ere are girls. Get yer laughing gear around this lot!'

'Aww, bless you, Ken,' whispered Lizzie. 'But I ain't got the cash to pay you for this lot.'

'Wouldn't dream of taking it Liz,' confided Ken. 'Anyway this was all Joyce's idea. I'd have gone for a tray of light ales if it was me.'

'Ken, you nightmare!' exclaimed Joyce, turning and glaring at him. 'Go back inside and get on with some bloody cleaning or something, will ya? We're busy cuddling babies here.'

'All right, all right. Stone me, keep yer hair on, sweetheart.' Ken winked at Lizzie, and set the tray of cups and saucers on the bench beside her. 'Drink up and enjoy ladies. Ice cream next, on the house! Ain't that so Antonio?'

'Si, Kennie. Ice-a-cream for the beautiful ladies. Vanilla, strawberry, and choc-o-late. On-na di 'ouse! '

The ladies burst in to a round of applause before settling on the lawn to enjoy the cool shade. Now fast asleep, James was being passed around from one lady to another with the care one might take handing fine porcelain. Lizzie watched the ice cream trickle down the sides of her cornet, catching each rivulet with a timely lick. She stretched her arms and tossed her head back to watch the white clouds dancing between the tall branches away up high as the warm breeze caressed her face. Oh, what a difference from Guys Victoria Ward. It was too stuffy and smelly, and there was never an open window to blow away the clouds of smoke from the chattering husbands in the waiting room. And never mind the stink of booze that came from them! How they even managed to stand on their own two feet was a complete mystery.

Joyce went around collecting the cups and saucers. Once done she rested the tray on the grass and sat down next to Lizzie. 'Look over there, Lizzie. Who's this dodgy-looking geezer coming toward us?' Lizzie raised her head and looked around. Free-wheeling down Queen Elizabeth Street Lizzie watched the figure of a stout gentleman dressed in police uniform on a bicycle, his legs outstretched like the stabilisers on a child's Tri-ang. Slowing to avoid a truck, with a squeal of worn-out brake pads, the mysterious rider picked up speed, pedalling towards the gathering, his police helmet raised above his head in salutation.

'Greetings, dear ladies!' announced the messenger.

Lizzie sprang up, smiling, waving her arms, her melting ice cream splashing the side of her face.

'Uncle George! Uncle! It's me, Lizzie!'

'Jezz woman, what's got into you!' Joyce giggled uncontrollably, licking her handkerchief and wiping the ice cream from Lizzie's face.

'It's George, not bloody Gary Cooper!'

'I know, I know,' protested Lizzie. 'But I haven't seen George since Tommy was banged up.'

With the grace of an elderly, black swan struggling against a neap tide, George manoeuvred all his weight onto one pedal to side-saddle into a landing space for his chariot. Realising gravity was not working in his favour on this occasion he abandoned his trickery with a clatter and threw the damn thing on the grass, staggering to maintain his balance.

Regaining his poise and readjusting his waistcoat and black tie, George, complete with cycle clips on both ankles holding the hem of each trouser leg at half-mast, swaggered up to Lizzie and put his arms around her, giving her a big bear hug.

'Lizzie my darling! You look fabulous! Radiant!'

'Oy, put her down you dirty ol' bugger,' cried one of the ladies. 'She's only just left 'ospital.'

'I know that you soppy mare, so it's only a tiny, little hug!'

The ladies burst into giggles as Lizzie swung on George's neck, nearly throttling him. 'Hold up, girl, steady on. I'm not as young as I used to be you know.'

'Uncle, it's so nice to see you. How have you been?'

'I've been very well my dear. And I assume this is James? God, he's beautiful,' exclaimed George, gazing down at one of the ladies cradling the sleeping cherub.

'I know,' Lizzie confessed. 'Obviously, he gets his good looks from his mother.'

More giggles.

George took Lizzie by her hand and nestled it in his arm. 'Lizzie, step over here with me for a moment, please. I need to have a word, you know, in private, please?' Lizzie glanced back at the ladies, now silent in expectation.

The lady holding James piped up. 'Go on Liz, we'll look after little'n. He's sound-o.'

'What's this about George?'

'I'm here on police business, Lizzie. Sorry and all that but it's important. Where can I get hold of Tommy please?'

Lizzie's smile disappeared. 'Oh gawd, what's he done now?'

'He ain't done nothing wrong at all my lovely. I just want a word, that's all.'

'He's in there,' nodded Lizzie towards the St John's Tavern door. 'He's having a beer with Frankie Miller.'

George moved closer to Lizzie, lowering his voice so only she could hear. 'You couldn't do us a favour, girl, could you?'

'What's up, George?'

'Just go in there and get Tommy for me. Get him out here. I don't want to cause a fuss by marching in there in uniform in front of that gobby bugger Frankie Miller. I just want a word. Tell him quietly I have a message for him from Detective Inspector Bellinger. He'll know what it's all about. It's fine, nothing to worry about.'

'You sure, George? This ain't another stitch-up, is it?'

Sensing Lizzie was getting uncomfortable, George took her in his arms again. 'Come on you, it's only police business. We all want you and Tommy to be happy together. God knows you've been through it lately. Believe it or not we're on his side this time. Snell's been transferred out of division so this has nothing to do with him.'

'Good riddance to that,' spat Lizzie. 'He's just a bad news bastard.' Lizzie hesitated. 'If you're sure, George, I'll go and get him.'

'Go on then, me dear, go get him for me. I'll make my way around the back by the barrels, so nobody will see us talking. Tell him I'll see him there in a minute.'

With that, Lizzie turned, strolled past Antonio and his ice cream trolley, crossed Weaver's Lane, opened the door and strode into the smoke of the St. John's Tavern.

'Come on then, Uncle. What's Bellinger wanting this time?' asked Tommy.

George took a cautionary look around checking for onlookers. 'He wants you to come and talk with him tomorrow. He's put the word on the street that you want to meet the Dennetts. They've got back through the grapevine that they'll be in The Swan and Sugarloaf on Parkers Row tomorrow at dinner time. D'you know it?'

'Yeah I know it. Piss-hole of a place right opposite the Catholic church.'

'They'll be expecting trouble, Tommy, you know that, yeah?'

'Yeah, and they'll get it.'

'Hold your horses, son, there's a plan of attack here. Bellinger wants you to go to Tower Bridge Station at 10.00 am tomorrow morning and ask for him at the desk. Constable Jordan will be hanging around the interview room so he'll take over once you get there. You'll be led into the interview room, so it will look like you're in for routine questioning if anyone gets inquisitive. Bellinger will be called for once you're there. Just don't be late. And please don't turn up smelling of booze. Everything will be explained once you get there. And one more thing, tell nobody. And I mean nobody, not even Lizzie.'

'So what do I tell Lizzie then?'

'Tell her there are certain parole conditions to be upheld, and this is just a routine check-up to ensure they're all in place. She'll be OK with that. Tell her I'll also be there and you'll be in my custody through the meeting until the afternoon, when we'll have you back in time for the pub to open.'

'Sounds fine to me, Uncle, but what about once I'm in the Sugarloaf. I'll be on my own won't I?'

'Ahhh, well ... that's exactly what Bellinger wants to talk to you about me lad!'

Chapter 10

The Setup

Constable Jordan raised his hand as Tommy walked through the main doors of Tower Bridge Police Station. 'Good mooring Tommy, how's Lizzie and the baby?'

'They're doing very well. They're back home now and loving the weather. I'm told I need to speak to Mr. Bellinger.'

Jordan put his hand on Tommy's shoulder and pointed to the interrogation room. 'You take a look inside there please Tommy, I'll let Detective Inspector Bellinger know you're here.'

Jordan led Tommy to the interrogation room and opened the door for him. 'There you go lad, there's someone in there waiting for you.'

Tommy entered the room to be met by a smiling Constable George Turner.

'Uncle! You said you'd be here.'

'Always a man of my word Tommy. Come in, come in. Take a seat,' offered George closing the door behind him. 'The others will be here shortly.'

Within minutes, the door reopened, and in bustled Bellinger, followed by Jordan. Full of benevolent smiles, Bellinger slapped his manila folder on the table and rubbed his hands in anticipation.

'Right then, everybody take a seat. Constable Jordan, if you wouldn't mind keeping an eye on the corridor outside, I don't want anyone hanging around ear-wigging.'

Jordan offered his customary, informal salute and, closing the door behind him, took up vigil outside.

'Right then Tommy, here's the situation. At 12.30 pm, two and half hours from now, you will walk into the Swan and Sugarloaf pub in Dockhead and buy yourself a pint. Don't look around. Just go straight to the counter and only talk to the barman. While he's serving you, tell him you're there to meet somebody called Dennett, pay for the drink and take a seat against the wall somewhere in the middle of the bar, in full view. You got that?'

'Yeah, I got that.'

'As far as the Dennetts are concerned, you have never seen their faces before, and it's important that you maintain this pretence. If they know you've been primed they're gonna want to know how and who primed you. We don't want to raise their suspicions. Clear?'

'Clear.'

'Right then. Now, please be aware that four of Constable Jordan's colleagues from the special branch will already be in the pub. They'll be in plain clothes, you'll neither know who they are nor what they do. Just be assured they're on your side, and if it kicks off, these guys are trained to act fast.'

'I'm with you, boss, but what happens when the Dennetts turn up? What am I expected to do?'

'They will no doubt want to know why you asked to see them. They're not daft so I'm guessing they'll be packing. They'll also expect you to be doing the same. Let them search you if they want to. As you'll be escorted directly from this office you'll be searched by us first to make sure you're clean. Trust me, neither us nor you will want this to go wrong.'

'Yeah, yeah, but what do I say? How does this pan out?'

'The Dennetts know you're Jack Baker's boy and they'll assume you're out for revenge. My guess is that they'll take a beat on you right from the very start and threaten you if you play up. Don't react! Just keep shtum. Let them take the lead.'

'So the idea is that eventually it kicks off, and Jordan's boys take over?'

'Pretty much, although I don't expect too much heat. The Dennetts are not on their own turf, so they'll want to be in and out with no fuss. Once they leave the pub they'll be met by reinforcements waiting outside. As soon as they get up to leave you make yourself scarce. Your job's then over; Jordan's boys do the rest.'

The black, unmarked saloon slowed on Tooley Street, passing Shad Thames and the River Neckinger. The car turned left into Mill Street and crawled along at a walking pace. The three occupants travelled in silence, alert but calm. As the vehicle approached the junction with Wolseley Street, it came to a halt. The hand brake cranked up into its locked position, and the engine was shut off.

Constable Jordan shifted in his seat and looked over his shoulder at Tommy. 'D'you know where you are now?'

'Yeah, I think so. If go right here along here, it comes out at the fire station, yeah?'

'That's right son,' answered Bellinger. 'Turn right again, and you're in Parkers Row. The pub's on the corner on the right. We'll wait here for ten minutes if it's alright with you. Once we're sure the coast is clear, you can get going.'

Tommy nodded. 'Got it.'

The next ten minutes ticked by. As if on cue, rain spots appeared on the windscreen, slowly at first, then more persistent. Jordan turned on the wipers, but without the engine running, they just jumped and scraped around, churning the rain and dust into a grey and brown paste, making vision impossible.

'This is fucking typical,' declared Bellinger. 'We need eyes Jim. Get out and clean that shit off will you please?'

'Yep, will do Sir.'

'Hold it, someone's coming.'

All three occupants fixed their eyes on an elderly gentleman dressed in tweed and trilby, strolling along the pavement to their left.

'Let this geezer go by first before anyone leaves this car.'

Jordan agreed. 'Understood Guv.'

The elderly gentleman passed the car and continued onward into the rain until he turned right and disappeared from view. A few minutes later, Jordan turned to Tommy.

'Showtime, Tommy,' declared Jordan. 'Over to you ol' son. Break a leg!'

Tommy stared back at the pair as he opened the car door. 'Fucking cheers, much appreciated,' he grinned.

Jordan chuckled, shaking his head in amusement. 'Get on with it, and good luck, son. Don't forget my boys are already in there, so you've got backup at all times. Just keep your wits about you.' Tommy nodded, a mixture of nervousness and determination etched on his face. He closed the car door with a solid thunk, muffled by the now persistent rain.

As Tommy took his first steps toward his destination, Jordan smoothly reversed the sleek black saloon back up Mill Street. The tyres splashed through shallow puddles, sending up small sprays of water. Upon reaching Dockhead, Jordan swung the car around, its engine purring to life as he accelerated. The vehicle sped away into the downpour, leaving Tommy to face his task alone – or so it seemed.

The Swan and Sugarloaf was uncommonly busy for a lunchtime. The pub was decked out with dark wooden panelling and stained glass windows that cast colourful patterns on the worn carpet. The imposing bar was made from polished oak, lined with brass railings and populated with beer pumps. The walls were adorned with an eclectic mix of memorabilia - black and white photographs of old Bermondsey, a dartboard, and advertisements for various ales and cigarettes.

A group of men in suits, some with their jackets draped over the backs of their chairs, ties slightly loosened, chatted about the latest football results. In the corner by the dartboard, a group of factory workers clad in overalls discussed their morning shift, faces flushed from the warmth of the pub and the effects of a few drinks. At the bar, a solitary, elderly gentleman dressed in tweed nursed his half-pint of mild, his trilby tipped back on his head, his pipe clenched between his teeth, emitting a thin stream of smoke that curled up through the haze towards the nicotine-stained ceiling. On the bar in front of him lay a crumpled copy of the Daily Express. He glanced up as he turned the pages to observe the bustling room with a seasoned eye.

The door to the saloon bar swung open as a young stranger walked in from the rain turning down his jacket collar. He approached the counter and ordered a pint. The barman looked him up and down as he cranked the beer pump.

'Summer's arrived then by the look of it, aye,' declared the barman from behind a handlebar moustache that bounced up and down as he spoke.

'Yeah,' replied the young stranger. 'Probably just a shower that's all.'

'Hope you're right sonny,' replied the moustache. 'That's one and tuppence, sure.'

Tommy turned over his change, picked out the required sum, and handed it to the barman. 'Tell me something. I'm here to meet a geezer by the name of Dennett. D'you know him?'

The barman counted the change and then looked back at Tommy.

'Dennett, you say? And what would youse be wanting with Mr. Dennett, young man?'

'Ah well, that's for me to know, ain't it.'

The barman punched in the till keys, threw the change in the drawer, and shoved it closed with a tinkle and a clang.

'Well now, seeing as ye've asked so politely, I'll be sure to inform Mr. Dennett of your arrival ... should I see him, that is.'

'Good idea. Cheers. I'll be sitting over there.' Tommy turned and walked over to a table adjacent to the door, resisting the temptation to look around. Moving the chairs around, he sat with his back to the wall, put his pint down on the table and, taking a deep breath, raised his head to take in the scenery.

The hands on the wall clock clunked away the passing minutes until the pub door opened again, and two thick-set men entered. Tommy watched as they ordered their drinks from the barman, who pointed over to Tommy upon handing them their change. The two men glanced his way briefly, then turned their attention back to the barman. Assuming these two gentlemen were the Dennetts, Tommy took the opportunity to take a good look around the bar. As his gaze wandered from table to table, he was drawn to a few individuals who raised their glasses to him in acknowledgement.

'Must be Jordan's men then. Thank God for that.'

Tommy took a sip from his pint as the two men at the bar turned to face him. They approached Tommy's table, grabbing two chairs in the process. They set them on either side of the table before him, taking up residence.

'Now then sonny, I hear you want to talk to me?'

Tommy put his glass on the table, not breaking eye contact with the speaker. 'Mr. Dennett, is it?'

'Aye, sonny, Liam Dennett at your service. The gentleman to my left is my brother Nedser. Nedser's not much for talking.'

'I'm Tommy Baker,' declared Tommy. 'I'm the son of the man you nearly topped last week.'

'How is the awl fella? Making a sound recovery?'

'Not really mate. The old man's in a bad way to be honest. They don't reckon he'll be out of Guys for a while. But don't worry; he's got a loyal and loving family around him, so I reckon things will be back to normal pretty soon, and he'll be out on the street doing business again. It's just a pity he seems to have lost his working cash. I was thinking you might know something about that.'

'You think?'

'Yeah, all the time. You should try it.'

Nedser raised his finger to Tommy's face shaking his head.

'Is that thing loaded, mate?'

'Aye, it is,' replied Nedser.

'Well, why don't you shove it up your arse and blow your fucking brains away.'

Liam grabbed Nedser's arm. 'Now, now, gentlemen. Let's play fair. We're all guests here, and the landlady's a friend of Mrs. Dennett. Keep it sweet.'

Nedser intervened. 'You keep your fekkin' gob shut, or I'll shut it for ye!'

'Well, if I did that, you won't hear what I've come here to tell you, will ya?'

'And what exactly is that?' asked Liam.

'I've come here to explain to you what is going to happen next. I'll say it slowly so it'll have time to sink in to your thick, fucking skulls.'

Liam smiled. 'This oughta be good. Let's have it.'

'There was a witness, a good friend of the family. This witness is prepared to stand up in court and testify it was you two that kicked the shit out of my dad and robbed him of his cash.'

'So?' questioned Liam. 'We're not afraid of some old biddy mouthing off. We can soon shut her up.' The Dennetts looked at each other and nodded in agreement.

'Ah yeah, the old school way,' chipped in Tommy. 'I wouldn't try that if I were you.'

'Why the fuck not,' demanded Liam.

'IF you do you'll have me and the rest of the family to deal with.'

'Oh fuck! Help!' chuckled Liam. 'Jesus save us!'

Amidst the lunchtime crowd, Tommy noticed a few women in smart skirts and blouses, probably office workers sharing a quick drink and a laugh with colleagues before heading back to work. Sensing tension at Tommy's table they quickly finished their drinks, gathered their belongings and headed out the door.

'Nedser, show young Tommy here what happens if our Holy work is interrupted in some way.' Nedser pulled back the left-hand flap of his jacket, revealing a handgun in a shoulder holster.

'Now, here's how I see it. If I hear any more shit like this we will take this to the next level. You wouldn't want to put your lovely girlfriend's and your bastard son's lives at risk would you?'

Tommy's face hardened holding eye contact with Liam. *'Say that again you cunt!'* he shouted standing up knocking his pint to the floor with a crash. Everybody in the bar froze, staring at Tommy's table. Then, a scream rang out from the back of the bar that took Tommy's attention. Nedser was standing next to him, his arm outstretched, his firearm in his hand, pointing at Tommy's head.

'Put that fekkin' thing away, you eejit!' bellowed Liam. 'You'll get us both knicked!'

The room turned to uproar as customers clambered to leave the bar. Liam grabbed Nedser's wrist, not fast enough to prevent a round from being fired into the pub wall.

'Come on, you oonchook, let's get the fuck out of here!' bellowed Liam pulling Nedser towards the door.

As the pair fled Jordan's men sprang to their feet. 'Freeze! Don't move!'

A man dressed in overalls shoved Tommy to the floor, and the remainder of Jordan's men sprang into action, rushing to the door in pursuit.

Outside the pub Liam and Nedser Dennett panicked. 'Come on, Nedser, scram. Those bastards are coppers, for sure. It's a set up!'

As the Dennetts ran past the fire station, the doors of the pub burst open, and Jordan's men emerged and took chase. With that a black saloon skidded around the corner and screeched to a halt in front of the Dennetts. A shot rang out, and Nedser fell to the floor. Jordan's men froze looking around them and seeing the barrel of a shotgun sticking out from the rear window of the black saloon.

Liam stared down at his brother lying in a pool of blood. 'Nedser, what have they done to ye?' cried Liam, dropping to his knees. He clutched Nedser's jacket and flipped him over on his back. The hole in Nedser's chest confirmed what Liam was dreading. There was no way Nedser could have survived.

The driver of the black saloon crunched the car into gear and lurched up to the pub's door as Tommy emerged. The rear door was flung open, and a voice bellowed from within.

'*Tommy, get in the car.*'

Tommy was rooted to the spot, dazed at the bloodshed.

'*Tommy, get in the fucking car now!*'

Liam rose to his feet in time to see Tommy staring at him across the vehicle's roof before he was bundled into the back, and the black saloon roared away..

Act 2

Chapter 11

Double Crossed

'Sir, I think you'll want to take this call. It's urgent,' Baines said, his voice taut with tension.

Bellinger looked up from his paperwork, brow furrowed. 'Who is it, Baines?'

'Constable Jordan, Sir. He says it can't wait.'

With a nod, Bellinger flicked the incoming call to his desk phone, his hand hovering over the receiver. He took a deep breath, steeling himself for whatever news was coming. 'Jordan, what's the news?' he asked, his tone clipped and professional.

Jordan's voice crackled through the line, heavy with gravity. 'It's not good, Sir. Nedser Dennett has been shot dead.'

'What!' Bellinger exclaimed, bolting upright in his chair. 'How in God's name did that happen? Who did it?'

'We don't know, Sir,' Jordan replied, his voice strained. 'Forensics are on their way now, but that's not all. Tommy Baker is missing.'

Bellinger's mind raced, connecting dots and considering implications. He gripped the phone tighter. 'How? Be brief, Jordan. Give me the facts.'

'One of the team called me from the pub telephone. The meeting between Tommy and the Dennetts kicked off. One of the Dennetts pulled a firearm and put a round in the wall. Apparently, when the Dennetts left the pub, a car pulled up from which a shot was fired, hitting Nedser in the chest. Tommy was bundled into the back, and the vehicle sped off.'

'So, who was in the car?'

'Two men, Sir. We don't know who the driver was, but our boys identified the guy in the back as Brem-Wilson from the Security Service.'

Brem-Wilson's black Austin Princess gunned along Dockhead, swung off right along Shad Thames, then turned left onto Queen Elizabeth Street. It slowed at the junction of Tower Bridge Road enough to jump the red light and, turning left, pulled up at the junction of Tooley Street adjacent to Tower Bridge Police Station.

'Now then, Tommy,' said Commander Brem-Wilson. 'You're probably wondering what all this is about. If the truth be known, you're a bit of a hero, but it won't seem like it right now. I'm dropping you back here at Tower Bridge nick so you can tell Bellinger all about what happened back there.'

Tommy glanced about, anticipating trouble. The driver was preoccupied with scanning the area.

'You can tell Bellinger, with your help, we have successfully eliminated one of the two most wanted IRA fundraisers in the South of England, and by doing so, the other will no doubt be excommunicated by his own people for his incompetence. You, however, have another role to perform. Because Liam Dennett saw you get into this car he will assume you are part of the plan to kill his brother. This means we, or MI5, are not in the frame that will enable us to continue our undercover investigations undetected. Clever isn't it?'

Tommy was utterly astounded by what he heard.

'Out you get now, Tommy. Go see Bellinger, give him my regards.' Brem-Wilson opened the door for him and shoved him into the street. Brem-Wilson slid the glass partition open. 'George, step on it, please.'

'Aye, aye, Sir.' The car dropped into gear and lurched forward as the door was pulled shut and the car sped away in the direction of the Bricklayers Arms.

Sergeant Baines stuck his head around Detective Inspector Bellinger's door, tapping on the glass as he did so, the sound echoing along the quiet hallway of the police station.

Bellinger looked up from his work. 'What is it, Baines.'

Baines entered the room. 'I've got Tommy Baker for you, Sir,' he announced, his voice tinged with a hint of surprise.

Bellinger reached for his telephone. 'Which line is he on?'

Before Baines could respond, Tommy shoved past him, his face contorted with anger. 'I'm not on a bloody line; I'm standing right here,' he barked, his voice raw with emotion.

The Detective Inspector hesitated, clearly taken aback by Tommy's unexpected presence. 'I, I... don't understand. Jordan said you were missing,' he stammered, his usual composure momentarily shaken.

Tommy's eyes flashed with a mixture of fury and exhaustion. 'Well, I'm back, and I'm pissed off!' he spat, slumping into the chair across from Bellinger's desk with a heavy thud.

Constable Jordan appeared in the doorway at that moment, his eyes darting nervously between Tommy and the Detective Inspector. The tension in the room was palpable.

'What on earth is going on, Tommy?' Bellinger inquired, leaning forward in his chair.

Tommy ran his fingers through his dishevelled hair, leaving it standing on end. His voice was rough and fatigued as he began to explain. 'That bastard Brem-Wilson's been taking me for a mug. Set me up to take the fall for Nedser Dennett's killing.'

'You?' exclaimed Bellinger, unable to hide his shock.

'Yes, and now his psycho brother Liam thinks I did it.' Tommy's voice shook with a mixture of anger and fear. 'Brem-Wilson made sure I was seen getting into the car from where the shot was fired. The bastard set me up good and proper.'

Jordan stepped forward, his face etched with concern. 'How did you get mixed up with Brem-Wilson, Tommy?' he asked, his voice barely above a whisper.

Tommy's eyes darted around the room, checking for eavesdroppers. 'Brem-Wilson interviewed me in Wandsworth. He was introduced by Rossi the governor. Said he needed my help to catch the Dennetts.

Never mentioned anything about killing. He played me for a fool, and now I'm in the shit.'

Bellinger leaned back in his seat, his expression grim. 'And now?' he prompted, dreading the answer.

Tommy's eyes blazed with a mixture of fear and determination. 'Now? Now Liam Dennett's going to come after me and mine. Lizzie and James are in danger because of that scheming bastard. He's put a target on my back and my family's too.'

'Oh ... God,' Bellinger muttered, the gravity of the situation sinking in.

'You don't get it,' Tommy snarled, his voice rising. 'If Liam Dennett's really IRA he won't stop at just me. He'll go after my family, Lizzie, my boy. And it's all because of your lot and your stupid games. You've put our lives at stake.'

Jordan's face paled, the implications of Tommy's words hitting him hard. 'We need to arrange protection for you. And for Lizzie and the baby. We can't let anything happen to them.'

Tommy slammed down his fist as Bellinger's pens and papers left the desk. 'You're damn right you do. And you'd better do it quick. I doubt Liam Dennett's the type to waste time. He's probably already planning his next move.'

Bellinger reached for his phone, his fingers trembling slightly. 'I'll make some calls. We'll get them to a safe house. It's the best we can do on short notice.'

'A safe house?' Tommy laughed bitterly, the sound devoid of any humour. 'That won't be enough. He found my old man, didn't he? He'll find them too, and when he does ...' He left the sentence hanging. The room fell silent, the unspoken threat hanging in the air. Bellinger dialled the number for HMP Wandsworth, his composure visibly wilting under the weight of the situation. A tense quiet descended upon the office, broken only by the steady drumming of Bellinger's fingernails on the desk. The phone rang twice before a recognizable voice answered on the other end.

'Rossi here,' came the clipped response.

'Detective Inspector Bellinger speaking,' he replied, his voice tight with contained anger. 'We need to talk about Tommy Baker.'

There was a moment of hesitation on the other end, a pause that spoke volumes. 'What about him?' Rossi finally asked, his tone cautious.

Bellinger's patience gave way. 'Cut the crap, Rossi,' he snarled, his voice low and dangerous. 'Why did Brem-Wilson use Baker as a stool pigeon to kill Nedser Dennett?'

'I... I'm not sure what you're talking about,' Rossi stuttered, his confidence leaving him.

'Don't play dumb with me,' Bellinger growled, his knuckles whitening as he gripped the phone tighter. 'Baker's sitting in my office right now, and he's told me everything. Every detail of your little arrangement.'

Tommy leaned in, his eyes flashing with rage. Bellinger held up a hand, stopping him before he could speak, knowing his temper could derail the entire conversation.

'Listen here, Rossi,' Bellinger continued, his voice dropping to a menacing whisper. 'A man is dead, and an innocent family is in danger. I want answers, and I want them now. No more games, no more lies.'

'Detective Inspector, I swear I didn't know anything about this,' Rossi pleaded, his voice cracking with what sounded like genuine fear. 'Brem-Wilson... he comes and goes as he pleases. I don't ask questions. I can't afford to.'

'You introduced them, didn't you?' Bellinger pressed, refusing to let up.

A heavy sigh crackled over the line, filled with resignation and perhaps a hint of remorse. 'Yes, but that's all. I swear it. Brem-Wilson said he needed to talk to Baker. I didn't know about any murder plot. You have to believe me.'

Bellinger's grip on the phone tightened. 'You expect me to believe that?' he spat, his voice dripping with disdain. 'You're the bloody governor! Nothing happens in that prison without you knowing!'

'It's the truth!' Rossi's voice rose in pitch, panic seeping into every word. 'Brem-Wilson... he's got connections. High up. Powerful people I can't even begin to name. I can't... I don't ask questions. Not if I want to keep my job, or worse.'

Tommy, who had been listening with growing fury, could no longer contain himself. He stood up abruptly, his chair scraping across the floor with a harsh screech. Before Bellinger could react, Tommy snatched the phone from his hand, his face contorted with rage.

'Listen here, you piece of shit,' Tommy snarled into the receiver, his voice trembling with barely contained violence. 'Your little introduction has put my family in danger. My girl, my baby boy. If anything happens to them, anything at all, I'm coming for you first. You hear me? I'll tear that prison apart brick by brick if I have to.'

Bellinger, recovering from his momentary surprise, quickly snatched the phone back. 'That's enough, Tommy,' he said firmly, shooting the young man a warning glance. He turned his attention back to Rossi, his voice cold and professional once more. 'I want every piece of information you have on Brem-Wilson's visits. Every date, every minute he spent in that prison. And if I find out you're lying, if you're holding anything back...'

'I'll give you everything,' Rossi said quickly, his words tumbling out in a rush. 'Every scrap of information I have. Just... please. You have to understand. I didn't know. I never meant for any of this to happen.'

Without another word, Bellinger slammed the phone down, his face flushed with anger and frustration. The silence followed was deafening, filled with unspoken accusations and the weight of lives hanging in the balance.

After a moment to collect himself, Bellinger turned to Jordan, his eyes narrowing with suspicion. 'What's Special Branch's involvement in this mess?' he demanded.

Jordan's face paled visibly, his usual confident demeanour crumbling under Bellinger's scrutiny. 'Sir, I swear I knew nothing about this,' he said, his voice barely above a whisper. 'We were just told to watch the Dennetts. That's all. Standard surveillance, nothing more.'

'And you expect me to believe that?' Bellinger's voice dripped with disbelief. 'After everything that's happened, you expect me to take that at face value?'

'It's the truth, Sir. I swear on my life,' Jordan insisted, his eyes wide with sincerity. 'We had no idea about Brem-Wilson's plans or Tommy's involvement. This is all news to me, just like it is to you.'

Bellinger rubbed his temples, feeling the beginnings of a headache. The situation was spiralling out of control, and he needed all the help he could get. 'Turner!' he shouted, his voice echoing through the office.

Moments later, Constable George Turner appeared at the door, his face a mixture of curiosity and concern. 'Sir?' he asked, sensing the tension in the room.

'Get in here. Close the door,' Bellinger ordered. 'We've got a situation. A bloody mess, to be precise.'

George entered and shut the door behind him. Bellinger laid out the facts in quick, concise sentences. 'We need to get Tommy, Lizzie and their baby out of the city. Fast. And this information doesn't leave this room, understood? If word gets out, we're all in deep trouble.'

Tommy leaned forward, his earlier anger replaced by a look of concern. 'What about my old man?' he asked, worry evident in his voice.

'I'll take care of your dad personally,' Bellinger nodded, his tone softening slightly. 'I'll put a surveillance team at Guy's Hospital. Round-the-clock protection. We need to keep you all away from Liam Dennett. He's out for blood, and we can't risk him finding any of you.'

The telephone ring suddenly shattered the tense atmosphere, making everyone jump. Bellinger grabbed the receiver, his movements sharp and agitated. 'Bellinger,' he barked into the mouthpiece.

'It's Rossi,' came the reply, the prison governor's voice sounding strained but determined. 'I've got an idea. A way to make things right.'

Bellinger's eyebrows rose in surprise and suspicion. 'Go on,' he said cautiously, unwilling to trust the man who had already caused so much trouble.

'My brother Lillo runs the management team at a holiday park near Caister-on-Sea in Norfolk,' Rossi explained quickly. 'I've just spoken to him. He's agreed to take in Tommy and his family if need be. Keep them hidden as long as necessary. It's remote, unexpected, and the last place anyone would think to look for them.'

Bellinger frowned, his mind racing through the possibilities and potential pitfalls. 'I don't like involving more people in this mess,' he said slowly. 'It's risky. Too many variables.'

'Lillo's reliable,' Rossi insisted. 'He's family. He won't say a word to anyone. You have my word on that.'

'And why should I trust you, Rossi?' Bellinger asked, his voice hard. 'After everything that's happened, why should I believe a single word out of your mouth?'

There was a pause on the other end of the line, and when Rossi spoke again, his voice was filled with a quiet determination. 'Because I want to make this right,' he said softly. 'I'll do whatever it takes to fix this mess. I know I've made mistakes, but I'm trying to make amends. Please, let me help.'

Bellinger's jaw tightened, his mind wrestling with the decision. 'If you're lying to us, Rossi,' he began, his voice low and threatening.

'I'm not,' Rossi cut in quickly. 'I swear on my life. On my children's lives. I'm telling you the truth.'

'Your life might not be worth much if this goes wrong,' Bellinger snarled, his patience wearing thin. 'I want your complete loyalty, Rossi.

No more secrets, no more games. If I find out you're holding anything back...'

'You have it,' Rossi said firmly. 'My complete loyalty. I promise. No secrets, no lies. I'll tell you everything I know, everything I learn. Just... let me help. Please.'

Bellinger hung up without another word, his mind made up. He turned to the others in the room, his face grim but determined. 'Rossi's offered a hideout,' he announced.

Tommy scoffed, his distrust evident in every line of his face. 'And we're supposed to trust him?' he asked incredulously. 'After everything he's done?'

'We don't have many options,' Bellinger said grimly, his eyes sweeping across the room. 'It's the best we've got right now. Sometimes, in this line of work, you have to take risks. Calculate odds. And right now, this is the best play we've got.'

The room fell silent as the weight of the decision settled over them all. They were walking a tightrope, with lives hanging in the balance. One wrong move, one misplaced trust, and everything could come crashing down around them. But they had to act, and they had to act now. The clock was ticking, and Liam Dennett was out there, plotting revenge. They couldn't afford to waste any more time.

Chapter 12

The Train from Liverpool Street

Bellinger leaned back in his chair, his mind racing with the situation's complexities. He glanced at Jordan and then back at Tommy, his gaze sharp and assessing. The weight of responsibility hung heavy in the air, almost palpable in the cramped office.

Bellinger abruptly rose to his feet and announced, 'I've just had a thought. Give us a moment, we'll be back shortly.' He exited the office, adding, 'Constable Jordan, please come with me.'

As promised, Bellinger and Jordan reappeared minutes later. 'Alright, here's the idea,' Bellinger said, his voice low and firm. 'Tommy, you're going home tonight. Pack bags for yourself, Lizzie, and the baby. Essentials only. Think carefully about what you'll need for an extended stay. Tomorrow morning, you'll meet Constable Jordan at Potters Fields.'

Jordan chimed in, his tone businesslike. 'Put the bags in the pram, make sure James is secure on top. Try to look as natural as possible, like any young family heading out for the day.'

'We'll have an unmarked van ready to go,' Bellinger continued, leaning forward slightly. 'Jordan and his men will drive you to Liverpool Street station. We'll plan the route to avoid any potential tails.'

Tommy's brow furrowed, lines of concern etching deeper into his forehead. 'Liverpool Street? Where are we going exactly?'

'You'll be catching the Down Holiday Camps Express,' Bellinger explained, his voice taking on a hint of reassurance. 'It's a Saturday train from London to Caister-on-Sea, with a few stops. It's a popular route for families, which should help you blend in. The journey terminates at Caister Camp Halt, where you'll be picked up and transferred to Caister Holiday Park.'

'And that's where we'll be staying? This holiday camp?' Tommy asked, scepticism evident in his voice. His hands fidgeted nervously on his lap.

Bellinger nodded, his expression grave. 'It's not the Ritz, I know, but it's our best option for keeping you safe. The camp is secluded enough to offer protection but public enough not to raise suspicions.'

Jordan leaned forward, his expression serious. 'Remember, Tommy. Act natural at all times. If anyone's watching, we want them to think you're just going on a family holiday. No furtive glances, no rushed movements. Just a young dad taking his family on a trip.'

'What about my dad?' Tommy's voice cracked slightly, betraying the emotional turmoil beneath his stoic exterior, his thoughts clearly racing to the life he was being asked to leave behind.

Bellinger's expression softened a rare show of empathy. 'We'll sort all that out, don't you worry. Your safety is the priority right now. We'll make sure your father understands, and we'll handle any work situation discreetly.'

Tommy took a deep breath, his chest rising and falling noticeably as he steeled himself. Then he nodded, resolve settling over his features. 'Alright. What time tomorrow?'

'Be at Potters Fields by 8:00 am sharp,' Jordan said, tapping his watch. 'The train leaves at 9:30. We'll need the extra time to ensure everything goes smoothly.'

Bellinger stood up, his chair scraping against the floor, signalling the end of the meeting. 'Go home, get some rest, Tommy. Tomorrow's going to be a long day. And remember, this is for your family's safety.'

As Tommy left the office, his footsteps echoing down the hallway, Bellinger turned to Jordan, his face etched with concern. 'Make sure everything's in place. We can't afford any mistakes. Not with what's at stake.'

Jordan nodded, his face grim, the weight of the operation settling on his shoulders. 'I'll handle it personally, Sir. We won't let you down.'

Before reaching for his phone, Bellinger waited until Tommy's footsteps faded down the hallway. He dialled the number he now knew by heart, drumming his fingers on the desk once more as he waited for an answer.

'Rossi,' a voice answered on the third ring.

'It's Bellinger. We've got movement on the Baker situation.' His voice was low and measured, careful not to let emotion seep through.

Rossi grunted, the sound of papers shuffling in the background. 'So soon. What's the plan?'

Bellinger leaned back in his chair, the leather creaking beneath him as he lowered his voice to barely above a whisper. 'I'm taking you up on the offer. We're sending Tommy and his family to Caister-on-Sea tomorrow. They'll be on the Down Holiday Camps Express, arriving at Caister Camp Halt around 2:00 pm.'

'Good,' agreed Rossi, a hint of relief in his tone. 'Not exactly a five-star getaway but it will do. At least they'll get some sea air.'

'It's remote enough for our purposes,' Bellinger retorted, his patience wearing thin. 'Can you arrange something with your brother? We need someone reliable on the ground.'

Rossi fell silent for a moment, the sound of his breathing the only indication he was still on the line. 'Yeah, I can get Lillo to pick them up. He's got connections in that area. Knows how to keep things quiet, too.'

'Good. Make sure he's discreet. We don't want to spook Tommy or draw any unwanted attention. This needs to look like a normal family holiday, nothing more.'

'Don't worry about Lillo,' Rossi said, a hint of pride in his voice. 'He knows how to handle these things. Been doing it for years.'

Bellinger pondered, his free hand toying with a pen on his desk. 'Alright. Keep me posted on any developments. If anything goes sideways, I want to know immediately.'

'Will do,' Rossi replied. 'Anything else I should know? Any special instructions for Lillo?'

'Just make sure Lillo understands the importance of this. We need Tommy and his family safe and under our control. No slip-ups, no loose ends.'

'Consider it done,' Rossi said, a chair scraping in the background. 'I'll call Lillo right after we hang up. He'll be ready.'

Bellinger ended the call, staring at the phone for a long moment, his reflection distorted in its shiny black surface. He hoped this plan would work. Too much was at stake to fail now. The Home Office was flying by the seat of its pants and the Dennett situation was proving to be a potential threat to everything. If they could just keep Tommy and his family under wraps, maybe they'd finally get the break they needed to bring the entire operation back on track.

The crisp morning air nipped at Tommy and Lizzie's faces as they sat on the park bench at Parsons Fields, their breaths forming small clouds in the chilly atmosphere. Their eyes darted nervously, scanning the quiet streets for their promised ride. James slumbered peacefully in his pram, his tiny chest rising and falling rhythmically, oblivious to the tension surrounding him. Beneath him, their meagre belongings lay hidden, a testament to the hasty nature of their departure. A large, battered van rumbled into view, its engine cutting through the quiet. It screeched to a halt nearby, the brakes protesting loudly, and Jordan leapt out, dressed in plain clothes that did little to disguise his authoritative demeanour. He nodded curtly at the young couple, his eyes constantly scanning their surroundings.

'Right, let's get you loaded up,' he muttered, his voice low and urgent. 'We don't have much time.'

The van's rear tarpaulin unfurled with a snap, revealing several pairs of hands reaching out to assist. Tommy lifted the pram's handles while Lizzie gathered their coats and a bag of essentials. With anticipation and fear, they clambered into the vehicle's dim interior, the metal floor clanging beneath their feet. Once settled among the other occupants - whose faces remained hidden in the shadows - the tarpaulin snapped back into place, plunging them into semi-darkness. The van lurched forward abruptly, causing everyone to sway as it carried its precious cargo into the unknown. The smell of diesel and sweat filled the cramped space, adding to the sense of unease.

Jordan's voice cut through the silence, sharp and commanding. 'Listen up, all of you. When we reach Liverpool Street Station, you'll need to separate. It's crucial for your safety.'

Lizzie's grip on Tommy's hand tightened. 'What? Why?' she asked, her voice trembling slightly. 'We've already left everything behind. Why can't we stay together?'

'Precaution,' Jordan replied tersely. 'Each of you will be accompanied by one of these officers until you board the train. Once you're on, you can reunite for the journey. But until then, we can't risk drawing attention.'

The rest of the ride passed in tense silence, broken only by the occasional whimper from James and the rumble of the van's engine. They followed Jordan's instructions to the letter at the station, parting ways with heavy hearts and lingering glances. Tommy found himself ushered through the bustling crowd, his escort's hand firm on his elbow, guiding him through the crowd of commuters and travellers until they reached their intended platform.

As the train's whistle pierced the air, a shrill harbinger of their impending departure, Tommy spotted Lizzie boarding a few cars down with James cradled protectively in her arms. Relief washed over him as he settled into his seat, his leg bouncing nervously as he waited for her to join him, his eyes never leaving the adjoining carriage door.

Scarcely had they reunited when the locomotive thundered into motion, spewing vapour and steam clouds that coiled about the concourse. Tommy leaned out the window, his eyes fixed on the receding platform of Liverpool Street Station. Through the haze, he watched as the familiar landmarks of London– the only home he'd ever known – began to fade into the distance. The dome of St. Paul's, the spires of the city's churches, and the looming silhouette of Tower Bridge all blurred together as the train picked up speed, carrying them towards an uncertain future. Tommy's mind raced with questions about what lay ahead on this unexpected journey, wondering if they would ever see the streets of London again.

Chapter 13

Caister Camp Halt

The train chugged along, its rhythmic clatter a soothing backdrop to their journey. Tommy cradled James, marvelling at the tiny fingers that wrapped around his own. He couldn't help but feel a surge of love and protectiveness for his newborn son. Lizzie returned from the guard's van, arms laden with supplies, her face flushed from the exertion.

'Here, love,' she whispered, passing Tommy a sandwich wrapped in greaseproof paper. 'Eat up. You need to keep your strength.'

James began to fuss as they munched on the simple fare, his tiny face scrunching up. Lizzie scooped him up with practiced ease, bottle at the ready. A few women across the aisle cooed and smiled at the baby, their eyes soft with maternal affection.

'What a darling,' one elderly lady remarked, her wrinkled face beaming. 'How old is the little cherub?'

'Just a couple of weeks,' Lizzie replied, her voice tinged with pride and a hint of exhaustion.

The train conductor appeared, his weathered face creasing into a smile as he checked their tickets. His uniform was slightly rumpled, evidence of a long shift. 'Everything alright here, folks?'

Lizzie nodded, adjusting James in her arms. 'Yes, thank you. We're off to my uncle's place in Norfolk for a holiday. A bit of fresh air, you know.'

'Oh? Whereabouts?' the conductor inquired, his curiosity piqued.

'Near Caister, I think. Never been before,' Lizzie admitted, a flicker of uncertainty crossing her face.

The conductor's eyebrows rose slightly as he took in their sparse luggage and the young family's dishevelled appearance. 'Bit of an odd time for a holiday, isn't it? With a newborn and all?'

Tommy cleared his throat, his mind racing. 'We're convalescing, actually. Doctor's orders.'

A flicker of suspicion crossed the conductor's face, but he nodded sympathetically, choosing not to pry further. 'I see. That must be your pram in the guard's van, then. Well, if you need anything, just give us a shout, alright? We'll do our best to make your journey comfortable.'

Tommy and Lizzie exchanged worried glances as he moved to the next compartment. They'd have to be more careful with their story and more consistent in their details. The rest of the journey passed quietly, the gentle rocking of the carriage lulling James to sleep. Tommy gazed out the window, watching the countryside race by, his mind filled with hope and trepidation about what lay ahead.

The train screeched to a stop at Caister Camp Halt station, its brakes hissing and releasing plumes of steam as it settled on the tracks. Stepping down from the guard's van Tommy and Lizzie gathered their meagre belongings, their movements slow and deliberate to avoid jostling the sleeping infant. The platform was nearly deserted, save for a few scattered passengers disembarking alongside them. The conductor appeared, his face creased with genuine concern, his weathered hands gripping the handrail as he descended from the carriage. 'Here, let me give you a hand with that,' he offered, his voice gruff but kind as he lifted the pram onto the platform with practiced ease.

'Thanks, mate,' Tommy mumbled, still wary of authority figures, his eyes darting nervously around the unfamiliar surroundings. He instinctively placed a protective hand on Lizzie's lower back, guiding her forward.

The conductor's eyes softened as he took in the young family's apprehensive expressions. 'Listen, I know it's not my place, but... be safe out there, alright? Have a nice time convalescing.' He paused, seeming to choose his next words carefully. 'This air, it'll do you good. Clean and fresh, not like London.'

Lizzie nodded, bouncing James gently in her arms, the baby stirring slightly at the change in atmosphere. 'That's kind of you,' she replied, a tentative smile playing at the corners of her mouth.

'My family's from these parts,' the conductor continued, his voice lowering as he leaned closer. 'Norfolk folk are good people. Kind-hearted. It's not London, mind you, but they've been through their share of troubles. American air bases and POW camps during the war, all sorts. They understand hardship.' His eyes crinkled at the corners, a lifetime of experiences etched into the lines of his face.

Tommy and Lizzie exchanged glances, a flicker of hope passing between them. They felt a slight relief wash over them for the first time since leaving London. Perhaps this new beginning wouldn't be as daunting as they had feared. As they handed their tickets to the collector at the gate, a dark-haired stranger approached, flanked by two rough-looking men. His wide grin seemed at odds with his companions' scowls, and something was unsettling about the way his eyes darted between Tommy and Lizzie. The couple instinctively drew closer together, their bodies tense with apprehension.

'Ah, you must be the Bakers!' The stranger's voice boomed across the platform, causing several nearby passengers to turn and stare. 'I'm Lillo Rossi. Welcome to Caister-on-Sea! I've come to take you to your new home.' His enthusiasm seemed forced, almost theatrical, as if he were performing for an invisible audience.

Tommy tensed, his hand instinctively reaching for Lizzie's, intertwining their fingers in a gesture of protection and solidarity. 'New home?' he asked, his voice laced with suspicion and a hint of fear. Lizzie squeezed his hand, her eyes scanning the unfamiliar faces around them.

Lillo waved dismissively, his gold rings catching the sunlight. 'Figure of speech, my friend. Come, your chariot awaits!' He gestured grandly towards the station's forecourt. With reluctance etched on their faces, they followed Lillo to the forecourt, the two rough-looking men falling into step behind them like silent sentinels. The gravel crunched ominously under their feet, each step taking them further from the relative safety of the train and into unknown territory. In the middle of the forecourt, a battered farm wagon that had been converted with enough seating for a dozen or so passengers stood waiting, its wooden sides weathered and splintered. The old horse hitched to it stamped its feet impatiently, sending up small dust clouds.

Tommy eyed the rickety vehicle sceptically, his hopes for a fresh start in Caister-on-Sea rapidly diminishing. 'Oh well,' he sighed, running a hand through his hair in resignation. 'At least we won't have to walk.' Lizzie nodded silently beside him, her face a mixture of exhaustion and trepidation as they prepared to embark on the next leg of their uncertain journey.

The rickety farm wagon lurched forward, its wooden wheels creaking in protest as they rolled over the uneven dirt road. The two rough-looking men perched on the coach box, their weathered faces set in grim determination as they guided the horse with practiced ease. Behind them, Lillo lounged against the side of the cart, his eyes darting between Tommy and Lizzie with unsettling interest. Tommy sat rigid, his arm protectively wrapped around Lizzie's shoulders. She cradled baby James close to her chest, her eyes fixed on the passing landscape. The pram, secured with frayed rope, swayed gently with each bump and jolt. As they rounded a bend, a makeshift road sign came into view. Crudely painted letters proclaimed 'Caister Holiday Park 5 miles.' The sign stood out against the backdrop of lush fields, a stark reminder of the war's lingering impact. Tommy recalled hearing about removing official road signs to thwart potential German infiltrators.

The afternoon sun hung low in the sky, casting long shadows across the arable farmland. Green wheat fields stretched as far as the eye could see, punctuated by the occasional copse of trees. Skylarks trilled overhead, their songs a stark contrast to the sombre mood in the cart. To the east, ominous clouds gathered on the horizon, their dark underbellies hinting at the possibility of rain. The air grew heavy with the promise of an impending storm, matching the tension that hung over the travellers. The steady clomp of the horse's hooves and the rhythmic rattle of the harness filled the air, accompanied by the cart's constant rumbling over the rough roads. Each jolt sent a shudder through the wooden frame, eliciting a soft whimper from James.

As they continued their journey, the landscape began to change. The neat rows of crops gave way to wilder, untamed grasslands. The smell of salt hung in the air, a reminder of the nearby sea and the uncertain future that awaited them.

Lillo Rossi leaned forward from the sides of the rickety wagon, his eyes glinting with a mix of nostalgia and something darker as he began to speak. 'You know, we weren't always here in Caister. My brother Ignazio and I came to London as poor Italian lads, barely more than children. Our pockets were empty, but our hearts were full of dreams and determination.'

Tommy and Lizzie exchanged wary glances, unsure of where Lillo's story was heading. The air around them seemed to thicken with anticipation.

'Our family scraped by, opening a little restaurant in the West End. It was a humble place, but the aroma of our mother's recipes filled the air and drew in customers. Ignazio, though, he had different ideas. Landed himself a job in the prison service.' Lillo's voice took on a hint of pride, his chest puffing out slightly. 'We were making our way, slowly but surely. Each day was a step forward, no matter how small.' He paused, looking skywards, his expression clouding like the storm that was rolling in over the Norfolk coast. 'Then 1940 hit. Italy declared war on Britain, and just like that, we were the enemy.' His fingers drummed against the wagon's wooden side, a nervous rhythm that spoke of old anxieties. 'Next thing we knew, we're in a POW camp right here in Norfolk. The world had turned upside down in the blink of an eye.'

ALWAYS EAT WHEN YOU ARE HUNGRY

Lizzie shifted James in her arms, her brow furrowed with concern. The baby cooed softly, oblivious to the weight of the conversation. 'That must have been awful,' she murmured, her voice laced with genuine sympathy. Her eyes searched Lillo's face for signs of lingering trauma.

Lillo shrugged, a sardonic smile playing on his lips. 'Could've been worse. We worked the land and sometimes stayed with local farmers. Produced food for the country that saw us as the enemy.' He chuckled, but there was no humour in the sound. It was a dry, hollow noise that seemed to echo the emptiness of those years. 'Ironic, isn't it? Here we were, labelled as threats, yet helping to feed the very nation that imprisoned us.'

Tommy nodded, his stance still guarded but his curiosity piqued. His eyes never left Lillo's face, studying every micro-expression. 'What happened after the war?' he asked, his voice low and measured.

'Ah, that's where it gets interesting,' Lillo replied, his eyes gleaming with a mix of mischief and something harder to define. 'Ignazio went back to the prison service. He climbed the ranks quickly with so many conscripted staff lost in the war. Became a warden, just like that.' He snapped his fingers for emphasis, the sharp sound cutting through the air. 'From prisoner to keeper in the blink of an eye. Life has a funny way of turning the tables.'

'And you?' Lizzie asked, her voice soft but steady. She leaned forward slightly, drawn into the narrative despite her initial wariness.

Lillo's grin widened, revealing teeth that seemed just a touch too white in the fading light. 'Me? I stayed here in Norfolk. I worked on the farms for a while with other former POWs. We tilled the same soil that had once been our prison, now our livelihood. But then Caister Holiday Park got its big makeover. Suddenly, they needed someone who knew how to manage staff and run kitchens.' He spread his arms wide, encompassing the camp around them. 'And here I am, putting all that restaurant experience to good use. From serving plates in a tiny London eatery to overseeing a bustling holiday destination. Who would have thought?'

Tommy's eyes narrowed slightly, his instincts kicking in. 'So you run the camp now?' he probed, his tone casual but his gaze intense.

'Staff manager,' Lillo corrected. 'I've got a network of old POW friends working in the kitchens and tending the gardens. We've made quite a little Italia here in Caister.' His words hung in the air, laden with unspoken implications. 'It's funny how things work out, isn't it? One moment, you're behind bars; the next, you're holding the keys. Life, my friends, is full of surprises.'

Tommy's eyes shifted to the darkening sky as Lillo's words faded. The once-blue expanse over the North Sea transformed, brooding clouds rolling in from the east like an invading army. The flat Norfolk landscape offered no shelter, exposing them to nature's whims. The air grew heavy with anticipation, the distant rumble of thunder echoing across the vast expanse. A gust of wind whipped across the group, carrying the scent of rain and salt. Tommy instinctively shuffled closer to Lizzie and James, eyes scanning the horizon. The storm's approach was relentless, promising a sudden onslaught of wind and rain. He could feel the electricity in the air, as if raising the hair on his neck. The two rough-looking men, their weathered faces etched with years of hard work and harsh elements, pulled up the horse, set the brake and sprang into action. Without a word, they unfurled a large tarpaulin. Their calloused hands worked quickly, securing the edges as the first fat droplets of rain fell, splattering against the dry ground with audible plops.

'Per favore, signorina,' one of the men growled, his gruff voice belying the gentleness with which he ushered Lizzie and baby James under the makeshift shelter. His companion helped her settle, ensuring the infant and the pram were protected from the storm. The men's movements were swift and sure, their bodies angled to shield the young mother and child from the intensifying wind. Tommy watched, a mix of surprise and admiration crossing his face. With their scarred knuckles and stern expressions, these men showed a tenderness he hadn't expected. They fussed over Lizzie and James, adjusting the tarpaulin to better shield them from the strengthening wind. Their rough hands, more accustomed to hard labour, now moved with surprising delicacy as they tucked the edges of the tarp around Lizzie's shoulders.

The storm hit in earnest, rain lashing against the ground and wind howling across the flat expanse. Yet under the tarpaulin, Lizzie and James remained dry, surrounded by the unexpected kindness of strangers. The makeshift shelter creaked and strained against the gale but held firm. Tommy felt a newfound respect for these rough characters. Their actions spoke louder than words, revealing a compassion that contrasted sharply with their tough exteriors. He nodded gratefully to the men, a silent acknowledgement of their kindness. At that moment, as the storm raged around them, Tommy realized that appearances could be deceiving and that even in this harsh world, there were still pockets of unexpected warmth and humanity.

Chapter 14

Caister Holiday Park

The tarpaulin snapped and billowed in the fierce wind but held fast against the onslaught of rain. Tommy, Lizzie, and James huddled beneath its protection, a thin barrier between them and nature's fury. The cart creaked and swayed, its wooden frame groaning under the strain of the gale. As quickly as it had arrived, the storm began to wane. The rain's intensity lessened, transitioning from a roar to a gentle patter. Suddenly, a shaft of golden light pierced through a break in the clouds, illuminating the sodden landscape. The fierce wind scattered the remaining clouds across the sky like leaves in autumn.

Tommy peered out from under the tarpaulin. The sun hung low on the horizon, its warm light casting long shadows across the windswept terrain. Lillo glanced at the sky, his expression a mix of relief and urgency. 'We should head back,' he said, his voice carrying a hint of tension. 'Night falls quickly here, and the camp awaits.'

The cart lurched forward, wheels crunching on the rain-soaked gravel. As they approached the holiday camp, the landscape transformed. Gorse bushes dotted the roadside, their yellow flowers a stark contrast to the muted greens and browns of the surrounding grasslands. The air grew thick with the scent of salt and seaweed, carried on the breeze from the nearby shore. In the distance, the first buildings of the camp came into view. Squat, utilitarian structures painted in cheerful colours stood out against the darkening sky. Light spilled from windows, warm and inviting after the storm's chill. The sound of laughter and music drifted on the wind, mingling with the rhythmic crash of waves on the nearby beach.

As they drew closer, more details emerged. A large sign, its paint slightly faded, proclaimed 'Caister Holiday Park' in bold letters. Families strolled along paths between the buildings, their voices a counterpoint to the persistent whisper of the sea. The cart rolled past a row of caravans, their metal sides gleaming in the last rays of sunlight. The coarse landscape gave way to manicured lawns and carefully tended flowerbeds. Yet beyond the camp's boundaries, the wild gorse and windswept grasslands served as a reminder of the untamed nature that surrounded them. The air, crisp and clean after the rain, carried the unmistakable tang of salt water, a constant presence that seemed to permeate every aspect of life in this coastal haven.

As the cart rumbled past the kitchen block and main dining hall, heads turned and eyebrows raised. The camp workers paused in their tasks, their faces mixed with curiosity and wariness. Some squinted against the fading light, trying to make out the newcomers huddled under the tarpaulin. Others whispered among themselves, speculation rippling through the small crowd like a stone cast into still water. The air was thick with the aroma of the evening meal being prepared, a tantalizing blend of herbs and roasted meat. A portly cook, his white apron stained with the day's labours, stepped out from the kitchen doorway. His eyes widened as he took in the sight of Tommy, Lizzie, and little James. A younger kitchen hand peered around him, her face a picture of surprise and intrigue. She clutched a large wooden spoon, momentarily forgetting the pot she'd left simmering on the stove.

The cart stopped near the staff accommodation area, its wheels crunching on the gravel path. Lillo hopped down with practiced ease, gesturing for Tommy and Lizzie to follow. The onlookers' expressions shifted as they emerged from beneath the tarpaulin, blinking in the brightness of the electric lamps that swung from overhead cables. Sympathy flickered across some faces, while others remained impassive, hardened perhaps by their own struggles. A few of the workers nudged each other, exchanging meaningful glances.

'This way,' Lillo said, leading them to a small, weathered building. The paint was peeling in places, revealing the weathered wood beneath, but it stood sturdy against the coastal winds. Inside, the accommodation was sparse but clean. A single bed dominated the tiny room, its metal frame painted white. A rickety table stood in one corner, flanked by two mismatched chairs. Thin curtains, faded to a pale blue, hung limply at the single window. A bare bulb dangled from the ceiling, casting a harsh light over the worn linoleum floor.

'It ain't much,' Lillo admitted, running a hand through his hair, 'but we'll have a double bed for you tomorrow. Make do for now, yeah? We'll rustle up a crib for the little one, too.'

Lizzie nodded, cradling James close as she surveyed their new home. The baby stirred in her arms, making soft cooing noises. Tommy's eyes darted around the room, taking in every detail. His gaze lingered on the window, noting its view of the camp and the sea beyond.

'Right then,' Lillo continued, clapping his hands together. 'Let me introduce you to the lads.' He beckoned to two men waiting outside. 'This here's Carmello and Domenico. Carlo and Dom for short.' The men stepped forward, filling the doorway with their presence. Carlo, a burly figure with hands like shovels, nodded curtly. His skin was deeply tanned, speaking of long hours working outdoors. Dom, leaner but no less intimidating, cracked a lopsided grin that didn't sit quite right on his stubbled chin. A long scar ran down one side of his face, a testament to a hard life.

'Welcome to paradise,' Dom smiled, his voice gruff with a hint of sarcasm. He gestured broadly at the cramped room and the camp beyond.

'It'll do,' grinned Tommy, holding out his hand in friendship. His eyes, however, remained alert, assessing the men before him. Lizzie shifted James in her arms, her expression a mixture of hope and apprehension as she faced this new chapter in their lives.

The storm returned with a vengeance, raging through the night with unrelenting fury. Wind and rain lashed against the thin walls of their tiny abode, creating a cacophony of noise that set Tommy and Lizzie on edge. The unfamiliar creaks and groans of the building added to their unease, making sleep elusive. Baby James, ever attuned to his parents' emotions, fussed more than usual, his cries piercing through the howling gale outside. The young couple did their best to comfort their son, but their own anxiety made it difficult to soothe him effectively. They whispered reassurances to each other and the baby, their voices barely audible above the tempest that seemed determined to shake their makeshift shelter to its very foundations.

As dawn finally broke, the storm subsided, leaving in its wake a damp chill that seeped into their bones. Tommy was the first to rise, his muscles stiff and aching from the cramped bed and the restless night. He padded over to the simple, worn sink in the corner of the room, splashing cold water on his face and running wet fingers through his tousled hair in an attempt to tame it. The icy water shocked him fully awake, a stark and unwelcome reminder of their new reality and the hardships that lay ahead.

Lizzie joined him moments later, cradling a whimpering James against her chest. They took turns at the sink, passing the lone, threadbare towel between them. The rough fabric scratched against their skin as they dried off, yet another stark reminder of their new circumstances and the comforts they had left behind. Tommy winced as he rubbed the coarse material over his face, longing for the softer comforts of their old life and the plush towels they had taken for granted.

'Here, let me take him,' Tommy offered, reaching out for James tenderly. Lizzie gratefully handed over the baby, seizing the opportunity to get dressed without the added challenge of holding their son. She rummaged through their meagre belongings, carefully pulling out clean clothes for all three. The limited selection of garments was yet another sign of how drastically their lives had changed in such a short time, and Lizzie found herself fighting back a wave of emotion as she sorted through their paltry wardrobe.

As Lizzie changed James' nappy, Tommy stepped outside their room, inhaling deeply to clear his head. The air was fresh and clean after the storm, carrying the invigorating tang of salt and seaweed that reminded him of their proximity to the coast. Puddles dotted the gravel path, reflecting the overcast sky like tiny, shimmering mirrors. He took a moment to survey their surroundings, trying to orient himself in this unfamiliar place that was now, for better or worse, their home.

Back inside the cramped room, Lizzie settled James into his pram, tucking a well-worn blanket around him lovingly. The baby cooed contentedly, his earlier fussiness forgotten in the comfort of his familiar surroundings. Tommy began to search the room, looking for something suitable to boil water in for their morning tea. The bare essentials of their new living space became glaringly apparent as he struggled to find even the most basic of kitchen items, his frustration mounting with each passing moment.

'Don't suppose you packed a kettle?' he asked, his voice tinged with a hint of desperation as he rifled through their bags, his frustration growing with each fruitless search.

Lizzie shook her head, a look of dismay crossing her face as the realization hit her. 'I brought tea leaves but completely forgot about the pot, let alone the kettle.' she admitted, her voice filled with regret. 'I was so focused on packing clothes and things for James that I completely overlooked it. I'm sorry, Tommy.'

Tommy frowned, running a hand through his hair in exasperation. 'Right. We'll have to sort that out soon,' he said, trying to keep the disappointment from his voice. He made a mental note to add it to their growing list of necessities they'd need to acquire in the coming days.

Just as the weight of their situation began to feel overwhelming, a sharp knock at the door interrupted their dilemma. Lillo's voice, thick with his Italian accent, called out from the other side, 'You two decent in there?' His tone carried a hint of amusement, lightening the mood slightly. Tommy moved to open the door and found Lillo standing there with a steaming mug in each hand, a welcome sight indeed. 'Thought you might need this,' he said, offering the tea with a knowing smile. The aroma of the hot beverage wafted through the air, a comforting reminder of home and normalcy in their current tumultuous situation.

'Cheers, mate,' Tommy nodded gratefully. He accepted the mug and felt its warmth seep into his cold hands, providing a small moment of respite from their troubles.

Lillo leaned casually against the doorframe, his keen eyes taking in the sparse room and its weary occupants. His gaze softened with sympathy as he observed their obvious discomfort. 'Listen,' he said, his voice taking on a more serious tone, 'there's a meeting in the main dining hall at 8:00 am. Everybody must attend, including you three.' He paused, then warmly said, 'Please come as my guests. I insist. It'll be a good chance to meet some of the others and get your bearings around here.'

The main dining hall buzzed with activity as the kitchen and grounds staff assembled, their voices creating a low hum of anticipation. The heavy wooden door creaked open, its weather-worn hinges protesting slightly, and Lillo stepped aside, ushering Tommy and Lizzie into the room. Lizzie pushed James' pram, her eyes wide with uncertainty as they crossed the threshold, the carriage wheels catching momentarily on the uneven floorboards. Suddenly, the hall erupted in applause, echoing off the high ceilings and stone walls. The unexpected reception startled Tommy and Lizzie, causing them to freeze momentarily in the doorway, their bodies tensing instinctively. Bewildered, they exchanged glances, unsure how to react to the warm welcome that seemed to engulf them from all sides.

A group of women, their faces alight with genuine warmth and curiosity, surged forward to surround Lizzie. They enveloped her in hugs, their arms strong and comforting, planting Mediterranean-style kisses on her cheeks that left traces of perfume and powder. Their rapid-fire greetings and exclamations of delight washed over Lizzie in a cacophony of accented English and snippets of Italian, leaving her flushed but smiling, her earlier apprehension melting away in the face of such enthusiastic hospitality.

James, nestled snugly in his pram, cooed happily at the sudden attention, his bright eyes darting from face to face. The warmth from the nearby kitchen block wafted through the hall, carrying the enticing aromas of garlic, tomatoes, and freshly baked bread, creating a cosy atmosphere that seemed to please the infant. He gurgled and waved his tiny fists, his chubby fingers grasping at the air, eliciting more coos and smiles from the women gathered around. One of the older ladies reached out to gently tickle his chin, causing him to giggle with delight.

Meanwhile, the men approached Tommy individually, forming an impromptu receiving line. Each removed his cap in a show of respect before firmly shaking Tommy's hand, their calloused palms testament to lives of hard work. Carlo and Dom were among them, their grips strong and their smiles genuine as they welcomed him to their ranks. Tommy found himself returning their grins, surprised by the ease with which he was accepted into this close-knit community.

Tommy and Lizzie's eyes met over the heads of their well-wishers, matching expressions of amazement and tentative joy on their faces. For the first time since their arrival, they allowed themselves to relax slightly, the tension in their shoulders easing as they were buoyed by the unexpected display of hospitality. It was as if a weight they hadn't realized they'd been carrying had suddenly been lifted.

Lillo stepped forward, commanding attention even before he made a sound. He clapped his hands sharply, the crisp report cutting through the chatter like a knife. A hush fell over the assembled crowd, conversations trailing off mid-sentence as all eyes turned to him. He stood tall, his posture radiating authority as he addressed the group, his voice carrying easily across the hall, clear and strong.

'Friends,' Lillo began, gesturing towards Tommy and Lizzie with a sweep of his arm, 'I'm pleased to announce that Tommy and Lizzie have come to join us for the summer.' He paused, allowing his words to sink in before continuing, his gaze sweeping across the faces of his staff. 'Lizzie will work with our kitchen staff, lending her skills to our culinary team.' A murmur of approval rippled through the crowd like a wave breaking on the shore. Several kitchen staff nodded enthusiastically, already envisioning the dishes they might create together. One of the older cooks stepped forward, patting Lizzie's arm reassuringly and whispering a few words of welcome.

'And Tommy,' Lillo continued, his voice rising slightly to regain the attention of those who had begun to whisper amongst themselves, 'will be joining our grounds crew as a groundsman.' More nods and smiles greeted this announcement, with a few men clapping Tommy on the back in a show of camaraderie. The groundskeepers, easily identifiable by their work-worn hands and sun-weathered faces, exchanged knowing glances.

Lillo cleared his throat, his gaze sweeping across the assembled crowd. The air grew thick with anticipation as he prepared to reveal more about Tommy's role. 'There's more to Tommy's position here than just groundskeeping,' he announced, his voice taking on a more serious tone. 'He's been recruited for a special purpose – to help reintegrate poor families who've suffered the loss of their parents during the war. These families, torn apart by conflict, need our support to rebuild their lives.'

Tommy and Lizzie swapped bewildered looks. The revelation caught them off guard, yet they played along now that the deception had been announced. Tommy noticed a flurry of activity as Lillo spoke among some workers. Several leaned close to their neighbours, speaking in hushed tones, their hands moving animatedly. It took him a moment to realize what was happening – they were translating Lillo's words into Italian. The soft murmur of their voices created an undercurrent beneath Lillo's speech, like a gentle stream flowing beneath the surface of a frozen river.

Lillo continued, unperturbed by the whispered translations. His eyes sparkled with determination as he elaborated, 'These families need a boost for their future lives, and Tommy's experience makes him uniquely qualified to assist them. His background in the docks, his understanding of the struggles faced by working-class families – these are invaluable assets in our mission.'

Tommy's eyebrows shot up in surprise, his mind racing to process this unexpected information. He hadn't been aware of this aspect of his new job, but he kept his face neutral, not wanting to give away his confusion. Inside, however, questions swirled like leaves caught in a whirlwind. What exactly did Lillo mean by 'reintegrate'? And how was he supposed to help these families?

As Lillo elaborated on the importance of this mission, Tommy observed the crowd more closely. He noticed that while some workers nodded along with Lillo's words, their eyes alight with understanding, others waited for the translations before reacting. Their faces would light up with comprehension only after the whispered Italian words reached their ears. It became clear that most staff couldn't speak English, creating a tapestry of languages and cultures within the estate's walls. The realization hit Tommy like a bucket of cold water, shocking him out of his complacency. He'd known he was stepping into a different world when he accepted this job, but the extent of it was only now becoming apparent. The mix of languages, the camaraderie among the workers, and the sense of purpose in Lillo's speech all painted a picture of a far more complex and interconnected community than he'd initially imagined. This wasn't just a job; it was an entire ecosystem, with its own rules and rhythms.

Lizzie squeezed his hand, her touch warm and reassuring, drawing his attention back to Lillo's words. The boss was wrapping up his speech, his voice filled with passion and conviction. His words

ALWAYS EAT WHEN YOU ARE HUNGRY

resonated through the room, touching each person present. 'Together, we can make a difference in these families' lives,' Lillo declared, his arms spread wide as if to embrace the entire gathering, 'Tommy here will be instrumental in that effort. His insights and experiences will be the key to unlocking a brighter future for those who have suffered so much.'

Additional cheers erupted, instigated by Lillo, who addressed his staff one last time. 'Alright folks, it's time to return to our duties. We've got visitors to care for, and holidaymakers will soon want their breakfast.'

The crowd erupted into another round of applause as they gradually dispersed, their sound swelling like a wave; Tommy felt the weight of expectation settle on his shoulders. It was a tangible thing, pressing down on him, making him acutely aware of the responsibility he'd just been handed. He'd come here looking for a fresh start, a chance to leave behind his troubled past and build something new. But it seemed he'd stumbled into something much bigger than himself, a cause that would require all of his skills and then some. As the applause washed over him, Tommy took a deep breath, steeling himself for the challenges ahead.

Lillo turned to Tommy and Lizzie. 'Right, you two, come with me, please, I have something for you.'

And with that, Lilo guided them into the now radiant sunlight, the dawn haze gradually dissipating amid the rhythmic roar of the surf breaking on the sandy shore.

Chapter 15

The Pledge

Tommy, Lizzie, and Lillo strolled along the beach path, the rhythmic crunch of their shoes on the sand mingling with the soothing sound of waves lapping at the shore. Lizzie pushed baby James in his pram, the little one cooing contentedly as the sea breeze ruffled his wispy hair. The morning sun cast a golden glow over the landscape. Seagulls wheeled overhead, their cries barely audible over the gentle roar of the surf.

'You know,' Lillo began, his eyes distant with memory, 'this reminds me of my first time in Norfolk. It was early July, back in 1940.'

Tommy glanced at him, curiosity piqued. 'Yeah? What brought you here then?'

Lillo chuckled a hint of nostalgia in his voice. 'Not exactly by choice. My brother and I were transported to Hempton Green camp in Pudding Norton. Manual labour and agricultural work, that was our lot.'

'Sounds rough,' Lizzie murmured, adjusting James's blanket.

'It was, at first,' Lillo nodded. 'But as the camp filled up, we got lucky. A local farmer took us in.'

Tommy raised an eyebrow. 'Just like that?'

'Just like that,' Lillo confirmed. 'They were kind people, always happy to accommodate. Even drove us to church every Sunday if we wished.' The trio paused momentarily, watching sandpipers scurry along the water's edge. Lillo's eyes softened as he continued, 'It was strange, you know? Being so far from home, in a country at war with my own. But those farmers... they showed us a kindness I'll never forget.'

Tommy nodded, his own thoughts turning to the unexpected kindness he'd encountered since his release. The sound of the waves washed away some of the tension he'd been carrying, leaving him feeling oddly at peace.

Lillo led Tommy, Lizzie, and baby James back towards the staff quarters. Tommy reached for the key in his pocket as they approached their assigned hut, but Lillo held up a hand. 'No, not here. Come with me, please.' Curious, Tommy and Lizzie exchanged glances but followed Lillo as he guided them to another chalet. Lillo produced a key and opened the door, gesturing for them to enter. Tommy's jaw dropped as they stepped inside. Their possessions, which they'd packed up before leaving London, were neatly laid on a double bed. The sight of their familiar belongings in this unfamiliar place stirred a mix of emotions in Tommy's chest.

Lizzie gasped softly, bouncing James on her hip as she entered the room. Her free hand reached out to touch the framed photo of the three of them, which she had carefully placed on the bedside table.

'This is...' she trailed off, unable to find the right words.

Tommy's eyes were drawn to the wardrobe, where he spotted newly pressed working clothes hanging neatly. He ran his fingers over the fabric, marvelling at the crisp feel of the uniforms. On the wall, a work rota caught his attention. Next to it were the names of their mentors for the first week. Tommy felt a flutter of nervousness in his stomach as he read the unfamiliar names, wondering what these people would be like.

'On the table,' Lillo said, breaking the silence. 'There's something for you both.'

Tommy turned to see an envelope on the small table by the window. He picked it up, noting that it was addressed to him and Lizzie. With slightly trembling fingers, he opened it. Inside were two pay packets – small manila envelopes with plastic windows exposing coins within. An array of notes poked from the top, secured by a sticky strip. Tommy's eyes widened as he realized what it was.

'An advance on your first week's wages,' Lillo explained, his voice warm. 'To be paid off as you work, of course.' Tommy looked up at Lillo, then at Lizzie, who was staring at the envelopes with surprise and relief. The weight of their new reality settled over them – they were here, they had a place to stay, work, and even cash in hand.

Lillo clapped his hands together, a warm smile spreading across his face. 'Well, now that you've settled in, why don't we get you both ready for some breakfast? The ladies in the kitchen have whipped up something special for you.' Tommy's stomach rumbled at the mention of food, reminding him how long it had been since his last proper meal. Lizzie nodded eagerly, adjusting James on her hip.

'That sounds wonderful,' she said, her voice filled with gratitude.

They took a few minutes to freshen up, Tommy once more splashing water on his face and running his fingers through his hair. Lizzie changed James's nappy and put him in a clean romper. As they left their new abode, the sea breeze carried the tantalizing aroma of bacon and eggs. Lillo led them across the holiday park, pointing out various attractions and facilities along the way. They passed colourful chalets, a bustling playground, and what looked like a small amusement area. Tommy tried to take it all in, his mind racing with possibilities for their new life here.

As they approached a large building, Lillo explained, 'This is where the staff dining room is. It's right next to the main kitchen unit.' They entered through a side door, and the smell of breakfast intensified. The dining room was simple but clean, with long tables and benches. A few staff members were seated, nursing cups of tea and chatting quietly. A booming voice called out to them in Italian as they walked in. Tommy recognized the rotund cook from the night before, his white uniform stretched tight across his ample belly. The man's face was red and jolly as he waved them over-enthusiastically.

'Venite, venite! Come, sit!' he called out, switching to heavily accented English. He gestured to a table set apart, with place settings for Tommy, Lizzie, and a crib for James. Tommy felt a lump in his throat at this unexpected welcome. He glanced at Lizzie, who looked equally moved by the gesture. They made their way to the table, Lillo following close behind.

Lillo leaned in close as they settled around the table, his voice dropping to a low murmur. The chef bustled away, giving them a moment of privacy. 'Listen carefully,' Lillo began, his eyes darting around to ensure no one was within earshot. 'You heard me tell the staff a story about why you're here. It's a cover they came up with back at Tower Bridge.'

Tommy and Lizzie exchanged glances, their curiosity piqued. Lizzie adjusted James on her lap as she leaned in to hear better.

'As far as anyone here knows, you're a young couple from London looking for a fresh start. Tommy, you've been struggling to find work in the city, and Lizzie, you're recovering from a difficult pregnancy. The story goes that I met you through a charity organization and offered you both jobs here as a chance to get back on your feet.'

Tommy nodded slowly, processing the information. It was close enough to the truth to be believable yet far enough from reality to protect them.

Lillo's expression grew serious. 'I want you both to understand something. No matter what happens, I will never reveal why you're here at Caister. Not to anyone. Not even to Carlo and Dom, my closest companions.'

Lizzie's eyes widened at this revelation. 'They don't know?' she whispered.

Lillo shook his head. 'No, they don't. And it's better that way. The fewer people who know the truth, the safer you'll be.'

Tommy felt a mix of gratitude and unease wash over him. On one hand, Lillo's commitment to their safety was reassuring. On the other, the need for such secrecy was a stark reminder of the danger they were potentially in. 'Thank you, Lillo,' Tommy said, his voice thick with emotion. 'We appreciate everything you're doing for us.'

Lillo waved off the thanks with a small smile. 'Just remember the story, and try to relax. You're here to start a new life, after all.' As Lillo finished explaining their cover story, he glanced at his watch and stood up. 'I'm afraid I must be going now,' he said, straightening his jacket. 'I have some business to attend to.'

Tommy and Lizzie nodded, still processing the information they'd just received.

'Today, I want you both to take it easy,' Lillo continued. 'Explore the camp, get to know your surroundings. It's important you feel comfortable here.' He paused, making sure he had their full attention. 'Tomorrow, you'll need to be at the entertainment hall by 9:00 am sharp. That's where you'll meet your mentors. They'll guide you through your first week, showing you the ropes until you're ready to handle your duties on your own.'

Lizzie bounced James gently on her knee. 'What about the baby?' she asked, a hint of worry in her voice.

Lillo's face softened. 'Ah, don't you worry about that, Elisabetta. My wife Sofia runs the crèche for the little ones. She'll take good care of James while you're working.' Tommy raised an eyebrow at the unfamiliar name. Lillo caught his look and chuckled. 'Oh, I almost forgot. From now on, you'll be using the Italian versions of your names. Tommy, you'll be Tommaso and Lizzie, you're Elisabetta. It's all part of blending in.' He leaned in closer, his voice dropping to a whisper. 'If any strangers or outsiders start asking questions, just pretend you don't speak English. Not everyone here does, so it won't raise suspicions.'

Tommy and Lizzie exchanged glances, both feeling a mix of excitement and nervousness at their new identities.

Lillo straightened up, a warm smile spreading across his face. 'Remember, we're like one big Italian family here. We look out for each other. You'll fit right in, I promise.'

With a final nod, Lillo turned to leave. As he reached the door, he looked back at the young couple. 'Enjoy your breakfast, and welcome to Caister-on-Sea.'

Lizzie glanced at Tommy and grinned, but her smile shifted when she noticed tears cascading down his cheeks. Lizzie piped up, clasping his palm. 'Come on, love, let's finish up and get some fresh air.'

Chapter 16

Discovery

The days melted into weeks as Tommy and Lizzie settled into their new life at Caister-on-Sea. The bustling holiday park became their world, a microcosm of Italian culture nestled on the English coast. The aroma of espresso and freshly baked bread wafted through the air, mingling with the salty sea breeze. Tommy found himself at home among the other Italian workers, their rapid-fire conversations and boisterous laughter a comforting reminder of his roots. He threw himself into his work, determined to make the most of this second chance.

On their days off, Tommy and Lizzie explored the expansive sandy beach, hand in hand, collecting an array of colourful seashells and smooth pebbles. The rhythmic sound of waves crashing against the shore washed away the memories of London's gritty streets and the hardships they'd left behind. They breathed in the crisp, salty air, feeling a sense of freedom they'd never known before. As they walked along the water's edge, their bare feet sinking into the damp sand, they dared to dream of a brighter future for themselves and little James. The vast horizon stretching before them seemed to promise endless possibilities, a stark contrast to the confining walls of their past.

One balmy evening, as they sat on their porch watching the sun dip below the horizon, Lizzie turned to Tommy. 'You know, I never thought I'd say this, but I'm glad we ended up here.' Tommy squeezed her hand. 'Me too, Liz. It's like we've found a little piece of Italy right here in England.'

Lizzie threw herself into learning Italian, her tongue stumbling over unfamiliar syllables. She'd practice in the kitchen, much to the amusement of her co-workers. 'Posso avere il sale, per favore?' she'd ask, grinning as they playfully corrected her pronunciation.

Baby James became the darling of the crèche. The Italian ladies cooed over him, pinching his chubby cheeks and declaring him 'bellissimo.' Lizzie's heart swelled with pride each time she picked him up, surrounded by a chorus of 'Ciao, piccolo James!'

Tommy found an unexpected friend in Dom, his mentor. They worked side by side, Dom's booming laugh echoing across the park as Tommy butchered yet another Italian phrase. 'Mamma mia, Tommaso!' Dom would exclaim, slapping his knee. 'You're hopeless, my friend!'

As May rolled in, bringing with it unpredictable weather, Tommy's skin bronzed under the intermittent sun. He often worked shirtless, much to Lizzie's delight and the giggling admiration of the female holidaymakers.

In their free moments, Tommy and Lizzie discovered the joy of swimming in the North Sea. They splashed in the surf, shrieking at the cold and marvelling at the vastness of the sea and the power of the waves.

The staff gatherings became a highlight of their new life. As dusk fell, they'd join their Italian colleagues on the beach. The air filled with the aroma of grilling fish and the melody of rapid-fire Italian conversation. Lizzie soaked up these new recipes, her cooking skills expanding beyond the usual British fare. Kitchen work was a whirlwind of activity. During meal times, Lizzie moved in a blur, serving hungry holidaymakers with a smile and a 'Buon appetito!' The lulls between meals were filled with the clatter of dishes and the hum of food preparation.

As weeks passed, Tommy and Lizzie found their rhythm. The work was hard but satisfying. They collapsed into bed each night, exhausted but content. Their efforts didn't go unnoticed - Lillo often stopped by with a word of praise, and their co-workers embraced them as part of the famiglia.

Saturday dawned bright and early, bringing with it the organized chaos of changeover day. Tommy watched from the sidelines as a stream of red-faced, reluctant holidaymakers queued to board the single-decker charabanc that transported them back to Caister Camp Halt, their luggage dragging behind them like stubborn children. The air was thick with excitement and melancholy, the bittersweet tang of endings and new beginnings. He observed the scene with a mixture of amusement and empathy, remembering his own childhood holidays and the inevitable return to reality. Families shuffled past, some still wearing their holiday smiles, others already donning the weary expressions of those anticipating the return to work and school. Suitcases bumped along the uneven path, overstuffed with souvenirs and sandy clothes, while parents corralled sleepy children and balanced precarious piles of beach gear.

Later that afternoon a fresh wave of arrivals flooded the camp. Children bounced and shrieked, their pent-up energy from the long train journey finally finding release. Parents juggled suitcases and picnic baskets, their faces a mix of excitement and exhaustion. The cacophony of voices, laughter, and the occasional wail of an overtired toddler filled the air. As Tommy helped direct the newcomers to reception, a face in the crowd caught his eye. The man looked familiar, too familiar for comfort. Tommy's mind raced, trying to place him. Was he from the old neighbourhood? A face from his past life? The possibility sent a chill down his spine, threatening to shatter the fragile peace he'd found in this new existence.

Swallowing hard, Tommy sought out Lillo. He found him near the dining hall, clipboard in hand, effortlessly managing the controlled chaos of check-in day. 'Lillo,' Tommy murmured, keeping his voice low and fighting to keep the tremor out of it. 'There's a bloke here. I think I've seen him from... before.'

Lillo's easy smile vanished, replaced by a look of intense focus. His eyes narrowed, scanning the crowd with newfound vigilance. 'Show me,' he said, his tone clipped and businesslike. Tommy pointed out the smartly dressed gentleman clutching his hat, who was currently registering at the front desk. Lillo studied him for a long moment, his expression unreadable. Tommy could almost see the gears turning behind his friend's eyes, weighing options and potential consequences.

'I'll look into it,' Lillo said finally, his voice barely above a whisper. 'Tomorrow at breakfast. For now, get lost somewhere and act normal. Don't draw attention to yourself.' He gave Tommy's shoulder a reassuring squeeze before melting into the crowd, leaving Tommy to wrestle with his growing unease.

The following morning, Tommy secured an inconspicuous position outside the dining hall while anticipating Lillo's cue. He busied himself with his usual tasks, hyper-aware of every guest approaching the main door. When the individual of interest entered and took his seat, Tommy discreetly signalled Lillo. With effortless grace, Lillo assumed responsibility for serving tea in that area; his actions relaxed and unrushed as Tommy resumed his regular duties.

'Good morning,' Lillo greeted the table warmly, pouring tea with practiced ease. 'I hope you're enjoying your stay so far. The weather's been particularly lovely, hasn't it?'

As Lillo turned to leave, the man's voice stopped him. 'Excuse me,' he said, his tone casual but with an undercurrent that set Lillo's nerves on edge, 'but could you tell me the name of that young fellow mowing the grass out there?'

Lillo glanced out the window, his face a mask of polite interest. 'Oh, I'm afraid I couldn't say,' he smiled apologetically. 'We hire quite a few casual workers, especially during the busy season. You understand how it is. Is there a particular reason you're asking?'

The man shrugged, his expression oddly blank. 'No reason, really. Just curious.' But something in his tone, a hint of recognition or suspicion, made Lillo skittish. Lillo turned to see Tommy looking at him from the putting green.

As he watched Lillo weave through the tables, Tommy couldn't shake the feeling that his past was catching up, threatening to unravel everything he'd worked so hard to build. Something about the stranger's manner tugged at Tommy's memory.

And who the hell wears tweed on their summer holiday?

The holidaymakers began to trickle out from the dining hall as the breakfast session ended. Children dragged their parents by the hand, keen to get on with whatever fun the day had in store. Elderly guests wandered to the cliff edge to take the wooden steps down to the beach and to walk along the shoreline. Tommy watched the exodus, his nerves still jangling from the arrival of the man in tweed. He busied himself trimming the edge of the putting green, all the while keeping a wary eye on the newcomer. The man lingered over his tea, seemingly in no hurry to join the crowd outside.

Lillo appeared at Tommy's elbow, his voice low. 'I've got a bad feeling about this gentlemen. We need to talk, but not here.'

Tommy nodded, his throat tight. 'Meet you on the jetty, by the boat in ten?'

'Make it five,' Lillo replied, then melted back into the bustle of the dining hall.

As Tommy made his way towards the Lillo's fishing launch, he couldn't shake the feeling of being watched. The carefree laughter of children playing on the nearby swings seemed to mock his growing unease. He made his way down the beach to the weathered hull, finding Lillo already there, pacing nervously.

'What'd you find out?' Tommy asked, his voice barely above a whisper.

Lillo ran a hand through his hair. 'Nothing concrete, but that bloke's been asking questions. Subtle-like, but he's fishing for information about you.'

Tommy's stomach dropped. 'Christ, Lillo. What if he's ...'

'Don't say it,' Lillo cut him off. 'We don't know anything for certain. But we need to be careful.'

As they spoke, the footsteps on the jetty made them both freeze. Tommy's heart pounded as he peered around the corner of the boat. The elderly gentleman from breakfast was strolling along the jetty, his gaze sweeping the beach as if searching for something—or someone.

Lillo's eyes darted between Tommy and the approaching figure. He hissed, 'Tommy, get into the boat and hide until this guy disappears. I'll ask him questions about where he's from and what he does for work. You keep quiet and out of sight.' Tommy nodded, his face pale. He slipped silently over the gunnels, pressing himself against the weathered wood. His heart hammered in his chest as he strained to hear what was happening.

Lillo stepped out onto the path, affecting a casual air. 'Buongiorno signore! Lovely day for a stroll, isn't it?'

The man in tweed came to a halt, his polished brogues crunching softly on the sandy platform. He removed his pipe with deliberate slowness, tapping it gently against the heel of his shoe to dislodge any loose tobacco. A smile played at the corners of his mouth, crinkling the weathered skin around his eyes. 'Indeed it is, young man,' he replied, his voice rich and cultured. He paused, inhaling deeply as if savouring the crisp morning air. 'Indeed it is. One can hardly ask for a finer day to be out and about, wouldn't you agree?'

'Sì, amico mio. A very fine day. And that's a smashing hat you've got there,' Lillo said, gesturing to the trilby. 'Don't see many of those around these parts.'

The man in tweed chuckled. 'No, I suppose not. It's a favourite of mine, though. Picked it up in London years ago.'

'London, eh?' Lillo's voice took on a note of interest. 'What brings you out to our little seaside town?'

'Oh, just looking for a bit of peace and quiet. Retirement, you know. And yourself? You work here at the park?'

Lillo nodded. 'That I do. Bit of this, bit of that. Whatever needs doing, really. What line of work were you in before retiring?'

The man's eyes twinkled. 'Civil service, my boy. Nothing too exciting, I'm afraid. Pushing papers, mostly.'

Beneath the protection of the hull, Tommy held his breath. The man in tweed's voice carried clearly in the morning air, and something about it set his teeth on edge. He pressed closer to the woodwork, willing himself to become invisible.

'Civil service, eh?' Lillo replied. 'Must've been interesting, working in London and all.'

'It had its moments,' the man said. His gaze drifted past Lillo, scanning the area. 'Say, you wouldn't happen to know a young man named Tommy Baker, would you? I believe he works here as well.'

Lillo's smile never faltered, but his eyes hardened. 'Can't say I do, sir. Lots of lads come and go in the season. Why're you looking for him?'

The man in tweed waved a hand dismissively. 'Oh, no reason in particular. Just thought I recognized the name from somewhere. Well, I won't keep you from your work. Enjoy the day, young man.'

With a tip of his trilby, the man in tweed turned and wandered back up the jetty towards the camp. Lillo watched him go, his fists clenched at his sides.

Chapter 17

The Man in Tweed

Lillo and Tommy burst into the chalet, his face flushed with urgency. Lizzie sprang up from the rickety chair, alarm etched across her features. 'We gotta move, now,' Lillo panted, his eyes wild. 'That bloke in the tweed — I checked with the staff. He's asking questions about Tommy. Specific questions.'

Lizzie cradled baby James closer to her chest, her face paling. 'What kind of questions?'

Tommy's jaw clenched. 'Doesn't matter. If he's asking, it ain't good.' He turned to Lillo. 'You sure he's not just some nosy tourist?'

Lillo shook his head vehemently. 'No way. The way he carries himself, the questions he's asking... Tommy, I think he might be police.'

'Shit,' Tommy hissed, running a hand through his hair. He paced the small room, mind racing. 'We can't stay here. If he's copper, there'll be more coming.'

Lillo shook his head, catching his breath. 'That tweed fella, asking about you by name. It doesn't make any sense. How does he know?'

'We need to figure out who knows we're here,' Tommy said, running a hand through his hair. 'It don't make sense. Only Bellinger's team, Rossi, and you should know.'

Lillo leaned in. 'Maybe someone talked. Or the Dennetts got wind somehow.'

'But how?' Lizzie pressed. 'We've been so careful.'

Tommy's jaw clenched. 'We need to reach out to London. Find out what's going on.'

'It's risky,' Lillo warned. 'If we start making calls, it could tip off the wrong people.'

'We ain't got much choice,' Tommy replied. 'If someone's looking for me, I need to know why.'

Lillo spoke. 'Maybe we need to get you out and hide somewhere else?'

Lizzie stood, her voice trembling. 'Where can we go? We've got James to think about.'

Tommy's gaze softened as it fell on his son. He crossed the room in two strides and gently touched Lizzie's shoulder. 'We'll figure it out, love.'

Lillo nodded towards the window. 'We have a boat which we use for fishing. You've seen it. We can be way down the coast before anyone notices we're gone.'

Tommy hesitated, looking between Lizzie and the baby. 'I don't know, Lillo. That's a big risk with James.'

'It's a bigger risk to stay,' Lillo countered. 'If that copper gets his hands on you, you'll be back in Wandsworth before sundown.'

The weight of the decision pressed down on Tommy's shoulders. He locked eyes with Lizzie, searching for an answer. 'We're not going,' she said firmly, surprising them both. 'I'm not running anymore, Tommy. Not down the coast, not to anywhere.' Lizzie touched Tommy's arm. 'What about your old mate, Frankie? The one who works down at the docks? He might've heard something.'

Tommy nodded slowly. 'Good thinking, Liz. Frankie's got his ear to the ground. If there's chatter, he'll know.'

'How do we contact him without raising suspicion?' Lillo asked.

Tommy thought for a moment. 'There's a phone box down by the crossroads. I'll call from there.'

Lizzie bit her lip. 'And if Frankie doesn't know anything?'

'Then we're back to square one,' Tommy sighed. 'But at least we'll know it ain't coming from our old haunts.'

Lillo stood up. 'I'll keep an eye on Mr Tweed, see if I can find out more about him without raising suspicion.'

Tommy nodded, a mix of relief and determination washing over him. 'Right then. Lillo, I need to get to the phone box now. What change do we have?'

'You're not going anywhere, my friend. Stay here out of view. I'll ring Ignazio from my office. Should I encounter Mr Tweed en route, I'll handle him with some Mediterranean charm.'

Tommy nodded. 'Be careful, Lillo. This fella seems sharp.'

As they prepared to put their plan into action, the weight of uncertainty hung heavy in the small chalet. The carefree days of their seaside escape seemed suddenly far away, replaced by the familiar tension of life on the edge. Tommy's fingers twitched nervously, his mind racing through all the possible outcomes. Lillo's usually jovial demeanour had turned serious, his eyes darting occasionally to the window as if expecting trouble to come knocking at any moment. The salty breeze that had once felt refreshing now carried an ominous chill, a stark reminder of how quickly their fortunes could change. The distant sound of waves crashing against the shore no longer soothed their nerves but instead served as a relentless countdown to the moment they'd have to face whatever fate awaited them beyond the safety of these wooden walls.

The phone on Ignazio's desk rang, its shrill tone cutting through the quiet of his office. He picked up the receiver, immediately recognizing his brother's voice, a mixture of comfort and concern washing over him.

'Lillo! How are you, fratello?' Ignazio's voice was warm, masking the sudden tension in his shoulders.

'Ignazio, good to hear your voice. How's the family?' Lillo's familiar cadence brought a smile to Ignazio's face despite the underlying worry.

The brothers exchanged pleasantries, catching up on recent events, their words dancing around the unspoken weight of their shared history. As the conversation flowed, Lillo's tone shifted subtly, a change Ignazio's keen ear didn't miss.

'You know, I was thinking about our time in the POW camp the other day,' Lillo said, his voice taking on a distant quality. 'Remember those long nights, huddled together for warmth? The way the cold seeped into our bones?'

Ignazio's brow furrowed, his grip tightening on the receiver. His brother rarely brought up their wartime experiences and never without good reason. 'Lillo, is everything alright? You sound... off. Like something's troubling you.'

'Oh, just feeling nostalgic, I suppose,' Lillo replied, his laugh a touch too forced. 'But since you ask, business at the holiday park has been interesting lately. We've had some unexpected visitors turn up unannounced. It's stirred up some old memories.'

Ignazio sat up straighter, his senses on high alert. The hairs on his neck stood up as he read between the lines of his brother's careful words. 'Unexpected visitors? What do you mean? Are you in some kind of danger?'

'Well, you know how it is,' Lillo continued his voice low and measured. 'Sometimes people show up without reservations. The thing is, we're getting quite full. We might need to accommodate some folks... elsewhere. The camp's bursting at the seams if you catch my drift. It's bringing back echoes of... less pleasant times.'

Ignazio's mind raced, decoding his brother's carefully chosen words. The implications sent a chill down his spine. 'I see. And these unexpected guests are causing problems? Are you safe?'

'Not exactly problems, but they're certainly keeping things lively,' Lillo replied, his tone guarded. 'Listen, Ignazio, I think it's best if we discuss this further. But not like this. Can you call me back on a secure line? And... it might be good to have Bellinger in on the call. We could use his... expertise.'

Ignazio's pulse quickened at the mention of Bellinger. Whatever was happening at Caister-on-Sea was serious enough to involve the Detective Inspector. As Lillo continued his tale about the man in tweed and his interest in Tommy, the pieces of the puzzle were starting to form a disturbing picture.

'Of course, Lillo. I'll arrange it right away,' Ignazio assured his brother, his mind already formulating plans. 'Stay safe, brother. And remember, we've weathered storms before.'

As Ignazio hung up the phone, his mind whirled with possibilities. What kind of trouble had found its way to their quiet seaside haven? And, more importantly, how deep did it go? The echoes of their past seemed to be rising once more, threatening the peace they had fought so hard to achieve. Ignazio picked up the telephone and switched to internal, his fingers moving with practiced efficiency. 'Maria, have the car ready and waiting for me outside. It's urgent. Ten minutes if you please,' he said, his tone commanding. The gravity of the situation weighed heavily on him, and he knew every second counted.

When he hung up, Ignazio took a deep breath, steeling himself for what was to come. Without hesitation, he dialled Bellinger's number, the detective's card lying on his desk like a harbinger of trouble. The phone rang once, twice, and Ignazio found himself hoping, against all odds, that this call might bring some clarity to the murky waters they were navigating.

Bellinger's phone rang, shattering the tense silence that had settled over his office. He snatched it up, his face hardening as he listened intently to the voice on the other end. The muscles in his jaw worked as he processed the information being relayed.

'Right, understood. I'll handle it,' Bellinger said, his tone clipped and businesslike. He hung up and jabbed at the intercom button, buzzing for Constable Jordan.

Within moments, Jordan appeared at the door, his expression a mix of curiosity and apprehension. 'Sir?' he inquired, standing at attention.

'Jordan, expect Warden Rossi at the front desk any minute now. Bring him straight to the incident room when he arrives. And get Baines and Turner here ASAP. This is urgent.'

'Yes, Sir,' Jordan nodded crisply, disappearing to carry out his orders.

Twenty minutes later, Warden Rossi strode into the station, his face etched with worry and his usually confident gait hurried. Jordan escorted him to the incident room, where Bellinger, Baines, and Turner were already waiting.

'George,' Bellinger addressed Turner, his tone softer but no less authoritative, 'keep watch at the door. Leave it slightly ajar so you can follow what's happening. We may need your input later.' George nodded silently, taking up his position with the quiet efficiency of a seasoned officer as Rossi settled into a chair, his fingers drumming a nervous tattoo on the table's polished surface.

'Alright, Rossi,' Bellinger leaned forward, his eyes sharp and penetrating. 'What's this about? We need every detail you can give us.'

Rossi took a deep breath, visibly steeling himself. 'I received a call from my brother, Lillo at Caister-on-Sea. He... he was speaking in code, but I understood him clearly enough. There are uninvited visitors at Caister asking questions. Probing questions that have him on edge.'

'Questions about what?' Baines interjected, his brow furrowed in concentration as he leaned in, hanging on every word.

Rossi's gaze flicked between them, a hint of fear in his eyes. 'About Tommy Baker. They seem particularly interested in his movements and connections.'

A heavy silence fell over the room. Bellinger's jaw tightened, his mind racing through the implications, considering and discarding possibilities at lightning speed.

'Did Lillo say who these visitors were?' he asked, his voice low and controlled, each word carefully measured.

Rossi shook his head, frustration evident in his features. 'No, he couldn't give specifics. The line wasn't secure. But he was rattled, and Lillo doesn't rattle easily. Whatever's happening up there, it's serious. These aren't your average busybodies or reporters.'

Bellinger exchanged a loaded glance with Jordan. 'This complicates things significantly. We need to know who's asking these questions and why they're suddenly so interested in Baker. This could upset the entire operation.'

'Could it be connected to the Dennetts?' Baines suggested, his voice barely above a whisper, mindful of the sensitive nature of their discussion.

Bellinger's eyes narrowed, his mind working overtime. 'Possibly. It's a connection we can't afford to ignore. But we can't jump to conclusions either. We need more information before we make any moves. One wrong step could blow this wide open.'

He turned back to Rossi, his gaze intense. 'Did Lillo say anything else? Any details about these visitors? Their appearance, accents, anything that might help us identify them?'

Rossi leaned forward, his voice lowering as if sharing a secret. 'Yes, Sir. Lillo mentioned a man dressed in tweed wearing a trilby. A pipe smoker. Well-spoken, cultured type. Said he was a civil servant, but he's retired now. Claimed he was only a pen pusher.'

Bellinger's eyes narrowed, his gaze sliding to Jordan. 'Ring any bells, Constable?'

Jordan straightened, his face lighting up with recognition. 'Yes, Sir. When we drove Tommy to meet the Dennetts at Dockhead, a gentleman dressed in tweed with a trilby walked past us. I couldn't make out any other details; it was raining hard at the time. If you remember, we waited until he was out of sight before we let Tommy out of the car.'

'Was he seen after that?' Bellinger pressed, his voice sharp.

Jordan shook his head, uncertainty creeping into his expression. 'I don't know, Sir.'

Bellinger's jaw tightened, his mind racing through the implications. He turned to Jordan, his voice clipped and authoritative. 'Check with the team in the pub, will you, Jordan? If there's any recollection of an elderly gentleman in tweed, I want to know.'

'Right away, Sir,' Jordan nodded, moving swiftly towards the door.

Bellinger's gaze swept the room, taking in the tense faces of Baines and Rossi. The pieces were starting to fall into place, but the picture they formed was far from clear. This mysterious man in tweed could be the key to unravelling the whole situation, or he could be another complication in an already tangled web.

Chapter 18

The Race

Jordan burst into Detective Inspector Bellinger's office, his breath coming in short gasps. He'd clearly sprinted back, urgency written across his features.

'The man in tweed, Sir,' he panted, gripping the doorframe. 'My guys confirm he was in the bar at the time of the incident.'

Bellinger's head snapped up, his eyes narrowing. In an instant, he was on his feet, palms flat on his desk as he leaned forward. 'Fuck me!' he barked, his voice cutting through the tension like a knife. 'Right. I want you, Jordan, and your Caister team as soon as possible. There's no point contacting local police; they'll turn up like a red flag at a bullfight.' He turned to Rossi, who'd gone pale at the sudden flurry of activity, his usual ruddy complexion now ashen. 'Rossi, get back to Lillo now. There's the phone. Tell him to get Tommy and his family out of sight. Don't care where just hidden. And make it quick; time's of the essence.'

Rossi nodded mutely, already fumbling for Bellinger's phone with trembling fingers. The gravity of the situation was not lost on him as he dialled in the numbers with unsteady hands.

Bellinger's piercing gaze swung back to Jordan, who stood at attention, awaiting orders, his posture rigid and eyes alert. 'Jordan, you'll have to make your own way to the camp. No buses, no lifts, just get there somehow, unannounced. And for God's sake, be discreet about it.'

Jordan's brow furrowed, a flicker of uncertainty crossing his features. 'Sir, how are we supposed to —'

'Figure it out, Constable,' Bellinger cut him off, his tone expecting no argument, sharp as a razor's edge. 'This is delicate work. We can't afford to tip our hand. You're on loan from Special Branch for a reason.

Use those skills. I don't care if you have to commandeer a bloody bicycle; just get there without raising suspicion.'

Jordan straightened, squaring his shoulders as a determined glint sparked in his eye. 'Understood, Sir. We'll make it happen. My team and I won't let you down.'

'Good man,' Bellinger nodded, a hint of approval in his stern expression. He then turned to address the room at large, his voice carrying with unmistakable authority. 'This is it, gentlemen. Whatever's brewing at Caister, it's coming to a head. We need to be on it now. Every second counts. Move!'

The room exploded into action, a controlled chaos of purpose and urgency. Rossi hunched over the phone, speaking in rapid, hushed tones, his free hand gesturing wildly as if to emphasise the gravity of his words. Jordan was already out the door, barking orders at his team, his voice fading as he strode down the hallway. Bellinger stood in the eye of the storm, his mind racing through contingencies and possibilities, mapping out strategies and potential pitfalls. The weight of command settled heavily on his shoulders, but he embraced it, knowing that the next few hours could make or break their entire operation.

Lillo's face tightened as he hung up the phone, his brother Ignazio's urgent message ringing in his ears. He wasted no time, striding purposefully across the campgrounds towards Tommy and Lizzie's chalet. The gravel crunched beneath his feet, and the salty sea breeze whipped at his hair, carrying with it a sense of impending danger.

'Tommy!' he called, rapping sharply on the door. 'We need to move, now!' His voice carried a note of urgency that cut through the ambient sounds of the holiday park.

Tommy yanked the door open, alarm flashing across his face. 'What's happening?' His eyes darted past Lillo, scanning the area behind him as if expecting to see trouble approaching.

'No time to explain fully,' Lillo said, his voice low and intense. He leaned in closer, his words barely above a whisper. 'We're moving you to my house. Jordan and his team are on their way, but we must immediately get you out of sight.' His eyes conveyed the gravity of the situation more than his words ever could.

Lizzie appeared behind Tommy, clutching James to her chest. The baby, sensing the tension, began to fuss quietly. 'What about our things?' she asked, her voice trembling slightly.

'Leave them,' Lillo ordered, his tone brooking no argument. 'We'll sort it later. Come on, quickly now.' He ushered them out of the chalet, his hand on Tommy's back, guiding them urgently.

They hurried across the camp, Lillo's eyes darting left and right, watching for any sign of the man in tweed. The usually cheerful holiday atmosphere felt oppressive now, and every laughing visitor was a potential threat.

Carlo and Dom were already waiting at his house, alert and ready. They stood like sentries, their bodies taut with anticipation. 'Carlo, Dom,' Lillo addressed them, his voice carrying the weight of command, 'you're on guard duty. Use your combat experience. Keep them safe at all costs.' The words hung in the air, heavy with implication. The two men nodded grimly, their eyes hardening with determination. They'd seen their share of action during the war, and this was a mission they took seriously. Their hands twitched muscle memory from years past coming to the fore.

'Inside, all of you,' Lillo urged, ushering Tommy, Lizzie, and James through the door. The baby whimpered softly, picking up on the tension around him. 'Stay away from windows. Carlo and Dom will keep watch. I'll coordinate with Jordan the moment he arrives.' His mind was already racing ahead, planning his next moves.

Tommy paused at the threshold, his hand on Lillo's arm. His eyes met Lillo's, filled with gratitude and a hint of fear. 'Lillo, thank you. For everything.'

Lillo gave a curt nod, his expression softening for a moment. The bond between them, forged in adversity, was evident in that brief exchange. 'We take care of our own, Tommy. Now go, stay safe.'

As the door closed behind them with a soft click, Lillo turned to face the camp, his mind racing with plans and contingencies. The sun was setting, casting long shadows across the grounds, adding to the sense of foreboding. The next few hours would be crucial, and he was determined to see them through, no matter what came their way. He took a deep breath, steeling himself for the challenges ahead, knowing that the safety of Tommy, Lizzie, and little James now rested squarely on his shoulders.

The following day, Lillo set his plan in motion with meticulous precision. He arranged for two of the camp's most reliable cleaners to attend to Tommy and Lizzie's belongings, instructing them to pack everything carefully and move it to his house. The cleaners arrived at their usual time, bustling into the chalet with their supplies, their arms laden with boxes and cleaning materials, ready to tackle the task at hand. As they began sorting through clothes and personal items, meticulously folding each garment and carefully wrapping fragile possessions, a shadow fell across the doorway, casting an ominous pall over the room. A man dressed in tweed, wearing a well-worn trilby and smoking a pipe, stood there blocking the sunlight. He smiled politely, the corners of his eyes crinkling, and introduced himself before stepping inside, the rich scent of tobacco wafting in with him, filling the small space with its aromatic presence.

The cleaning ladies exchanged uneasy glances, their hands momentarily stilling in their work, but the elderly gentleman paid them no mind, his focus elsewhere. He strode purposefully to the sideboard, his eyes fixed on a framed photograph among other knick-knacks and souvenirs, a frozen moment captured behind glass. Without hesitation, he plucked it from its place and slipped it into his jacket pocket with a practiced motion.

The cleaners watched, wide-eyed and silent, as the man in tweed tipped his hat to them, his disposition calm and unperturbed. 'Good day, ladies,' he said warmly, replacing his trilby with a flourish that seemed at odds with his mysterious behaviour. He turned and walked out of the chalet, his footsteps crunching on the gravel outside, leaving a palpable sense of unease that seemed to linger like the fading scent of his pipe smoke, a reminder of the strange encounter.

The two women stared after him, their faces a mixture of confusion and exasperation, their minds racing with questions they dared not voice aloud. They exchanged bewildered looks, their hands frozen mid-task as they tried to process what had just happened. The sudden intrusion disrupted their routine, leaving them feeling off-kilter and unsure how to proceed with their assigned task. They stood there for a moment, the silence broken only by the distant sounds of the holiday park, before slowly resuming their work, casting frequent glances at the door as if expecting the mysterious man to return at any moment.

Chapter 19

The Call

The man in tweed stepped into the phone box at the crossroads, his fingers dialling the number written on his copy of the Daily Express. As the connection crackled to life, he spoke in hushed tones, his voice barely audible above the distant sounds of holidaymakers and the sea breeze rustling through nearby trees.

'Yes, Commander, I have located Tommy Baker, and I have his photograph in front of me.' He paused, listening intently to the voice on the other end, his free hand unconsciously adjusting the brim of his trilby hat in the phone box mirror. 'Indeed, he's living in a chalet on the holiday park and working as a gardener.'

The man's eyes darted around, scanning the area with practiced vigilance, ensuring no one was within earshot as he continued. 'It will be an easy target to eliminate. The holiday park falls silent after 11:00 pm, lights out with everyone usually tucked up in their beds. There should be no trouble being spotted after dark. The layout of the park provides ample cover and multiple escape routes.'

He nodded, responding to an unseen request, his fingers tightening around the receiver. 'Of course, Commander. I'll bring the photograph back with me. Rest assured, it won't fall into the wrong hands.'

After a brief exchange, during which he received final instructions and confirmations, the man in tweed hung up and exited the phone box. He retrieved his worn leather suitcase, carefully tucking the photograph into his jacket pocket. He made his way to the wooden bench by the bus stop and settled in, his keen eyes never ceasing their surveillance of the surroundings. As he waited, he pondered the fate of Thomas Baker and how Commander Brem-Wilson's plans would soon shatter the man's newfound peace. He produced his well-worn copy of the Daily Express from under his arm, and turned to the sports pages.

As he began to read, he lit his pipe, puffs of smoke curling around him in the warm breeze. Moments later, he pulled out a pocket watch, its silver-polished surface glinting in the sunlight. As he checked the time, a black saloon car rounded the corner, pulling up smoothly beside him.

'Perfect timing,' the man in tweed declared, a hint of satisfaction in his voice. He rose from the bench, tossing his suitcase and newspaper into the back seat before sliding into the passenger side. The car door shut with a solid thunk, and the vehicle pulled away, leaving only a lingering trace of pipe smoke behind.

Lillo's house bustled with activity as the cleaning ladies arrived, their carts rattling along the gravel path. A gentle tap at the back door announced their arrival. Lillo strode over, his face a mask of calm determination, and swung the door open.

'Come in, quickly now,' he ushered them inside, his eyes darting left and right to ensure no one had followed.

The women shuffled into the back room, whereupon Tommy and Lizzie hurriedly unpacked their belongings. Baby James lay in a makeshift crib, blissfully unaware of the tension surrounding him. Lizzie looked up from her unpacking, a frown creasing her brow. 'Tommy, have you seen that photograph? You know, the one of us holding James?'

Tommy paused, his hand hovering over a pile of clothes. 'It was on the sideboard, wasn't it?'

They began to search, rifling through bags and boxes with increasing urgency.

'It's not here,' Lizzie said, her voice tight with worry. 'I wanted to keep it close, to remind us of home.'

Tommy sat beside her, wrapping an arm around her shoulders. 'We'll find it, Liz. It's got to be somewhere.' Tommy turned to the cleaning ladies, his voice urgent. 'The photograph, did you pack it?'

The women exchanged confused glances, their limited English failing them at this crucial moment. They shook their heads, muttering in Italian.

'Lillo!' Tommy called out, frustration evident in his voice. 'We need your help.'

Lillo hurried over, his brow furrowed with concern. He spoke to the cleaning ladies in rapid Italian, his gestures animated as he described the missing photograph. The women's eyes widened with recognition, and they began to speak at once, their voices overlapping. Lillo held up a hand, silencing them, and listened intently as one of the women explained. His face grew grave as he turned to Tommy and Lizzie. 'They say a man in tweed came to the chalet,' Lillo said, his voice low. 'They thought he was a friend of yours, Tommy. Thought you'd asked him to fetch the photograph.'

Tommy's face paled. 'And they gave it to him?'

Lillo nodded, then returned to the cleaning ladies, asking more questions. After a brief exchange, he sighed heavily. 'They didn't know any better, Tommy,' Lillo explained. 'They thought he was sent by me or you. We can't blame them for this.'

Lizzie clutched James closer, her eyes wide with fear. 'Who was he, Tommy? What does he want with our picture?'

Tommy shook his head, his jaw clenched. 'I don't know, but it can't be good.'

Lillo's expression hardened. 'I need to make a call. Stay here, all of you.'

He rushed from the room, leaving Tommy and Lizzie to comfort the distressed cleaning ladies. Lillo snatched up the phone in his office, his fingers flying over the rotary dial. 'Bellinger,' he barked when the line connected. 'We have a situation. The man in tweed, he's been here. He took a photograph of Tommy, Lizzie, and the baby.'

Commander Brem-Wilson sat behind his imposing oak desk, his office a bastion of order and authority. The room exuded an air of power, with its dark wood panelling and shelves lined with leather-bound books. The phone on his desk rang, its shrill tone cutting through the silence. He picked up the receiver, his voice crisp and businesslike.

'Brem-Wilson speaking.' He listened intently, his eyes narrowing as the man in tweed delivered his report. The Commander's free hand tapped rhythmically on the polished surface of his desk. 'Excellent. Can you confirm the subject's identity beyond doubt?' he asked, his tone measured but expectant.

'Yes, Commander, I have located Tommy Baker, and I have his photograph here in front of me,' came the reply, crackling through the telephone line.

Brem-Wilson nodded, satisfied. A slight smile played at the corners of his mouth, barely perceptible. 'Very good. Can you also confirm the subject's current status and location?'

'Indeed, he's living in a chalet on the holiday park and working as a gardener,' the man in tweed reported, his voice steady and confident.

The Commander's lips finally curved into a thin smile, a predatory gleam in his eyes. 'I see. Has the subject made contact with any known associates or suspicious individuals?'

He listened to the response, jotting down notes on a pad beside him. His pen moved swiftly across the paper, capturing every detail.

'And what of his family? Are they with him?' Brem-Wilson pressed, his curiosity piqued.

'Indeed they are Commander. All three live in the same chalet, No. 234 along Beach Boulevard,' came the reply.

Brem-Wilson's mind raced, considering the implications of this new development. After a moment's contemplation, he continued his questioning. 'Understood. Have you observed any unusual activity or behaviour that might suggest he's aware of our surveillance?'

'None,' the man in tweed answered succinctly.

Brem-Wilson's pen paused as he absorbed the information. He leaned back in his chair, the leather creaking softly beneath him. 'Well that's that then. Thank you, your work is done. Remember, discretion is paramount. We cannot afford any mistakes at this stage.'

His gaze drifted to the window as he spoke, where the grey London sky loomed ominously. The new development of the operation settled on his shoulders, a burden he bore with grim determination. 'Thank you Tommy Baker,' he murmured to himself. 'You have one more assignment, and your task will be over. One way or another.'

The Earl of Derby pub on Grange Road buzzed with the usual evening crowd. Smoke hung thick in the air, mingling with the scent of stale beer. The cacophony of voices, clinking glasses, and occasional bursts of raucous laughter filled the space. Liam Dennett pushed through the heavy wooden door, its hinges creaking in protest. His sharp, alert eyes scanned the dimly lit room, adjusting to the murky atmosphere.

He went to the counter and bought himself a pint of mild. Looking around he identified his contact in a secluded corner booth, dressed in tweed, his face obscured by shadows cast by the dim lamp overhead. Liam made his way over, weaving between patrons and battered tables. The contact looked up as Liam approached, saying nothing. A plain manila envelope slid across the sticky tabletop, leaving a trail in the condensation from a nearby pint glass. Without a word, the man in tweed stood and walked away, leaving Liam alone with the mysterious package. The contact's abrupt departure went unnoticed by the other patrons, who were too engrossed in their conversations and drinks.

Liam's fingers trembled as he picked up the envelope, its weight surprisingly light for something potentially significant. It was unmarked, and no writing or addressee was seen. He glanced around, ensuring no one was watching, then carefully opened it. Inside, he found a single photograph, its glossy surface catching the dim light. His breath caught in his throat as he recognised the subjects: Tommy Baker,

Lizzie, and their baby James. The young family smiled at the camera, looking carefree and happy. Tommy's arm was wrapped protectively around Lizzie's shoulders, while she cradled little James against her chest. The background suggested a park or playground.

Liam flipped the photo over, his eyes widening as he read the neat handwriting on the back. The blue ink stood out starkly against the white paper:

Caister-on-Sea Holiday Park
Chalet No. 234
Beach Boulevard

He stared at the words, a mix of emotions washing over him. Revenge for his brother's death was within reach, tantalisingly close. The faces of Tommy and his family burned into his memory, a stark contrast to the grief and anger that had consumed him since Nedser's passing. Liam tucked the photo back into the envelope and slipped it into his jacket pocket, patting it once to ensure its safety.

He stood, drained the rest of his pint in one long gulp, and walked out of the pub into the cool London night. The street outside was quiet compared to the pub's interior, and Liam took a deep breath of the crisp air. His mind raced with plans and possibilities as he melted into the shadows, disappearing into the labyrinth of Bermondsey's streets.

Chapter 20

Enniskillen, Co Fermanagh

Liam slipped into the red telephone box on the corner of Grange Road, the door creaking shut behind him. The cramped space smelled of cigarette smoke and stale urine. He fished some coins out of his pocket, slotted them into the pay phone and dialled the number, hands shaking slightly.

After a few rings, a quiet voice answered. 'Yeah?'

'Daddie, it's Liam,' he said, trying to keep his tone even and respectful. 'I've found Tommy Baker. I know where he's hiding with his family.'

His father was silent for a moment. When he spoke, his voice was low and dangerous. 'Where?'

Liam glanced around nervously even though he was alone in the box. 'They're at a holiday park. Caister-on-Sea. Got them in a photo and everything. Chalet 234 on Beach Boulevard.'

'I see,' his father said. 'And how exactly did you come by this information?'

Liam hesitated. He didn't want to admit to his father that he'd been anonymously tipped off. 'I have my sources, Da,' he lied. 'But it's legit, Daddie. I know it's him and his missus and the babe.'

His father grunted. 'Well now. Seems we've got an opportunity here to settle some unfinished business with Mr Baker, doesn't it, son?'

'I want to make this right, Da,' Liam said earnestly. 'For Nedser. And for the family.'

'Do you now?' His father's tone was mocking. 'Because the way I heard it, you bungled things properly with the Baker business. Got Nedser killed and yourself nearly moidered, isn't that right?'

Liam flushed. 'I'm sorry, Da. I know we messed up. But I can fix this. I just need some help.'

'Oh, you'll get your help, son,' his father said coldly. 'I'm sending one of my best boys over to see you. I'm sending Malone. You remember Malone, don't you?'

Liam's blood ran cold. Malone was ruthless and known for his cruelty. 'Yes Da,' he said quietly.

'Good. You will meet Malone off the Birkenhead train at Paddington in two days. And don't mess this up, Liam. You hear me?'

'I hear you, Da,' Liam said. 'I won't let you down again.'

The line went dead. Liam slowly hung up the receiver, his father's warning echoing in his ears. He had two days to prepare before Malone arrived. Two days before Tommy Baker's fate would be sealed.

Act 3

Chapter 21

The Journey

The ferry from Belfast to Liverpool slowly pulled into the Birkenhead Terminal, letting out a long blast of its horn to signal its arrival. Passengers began gathering their belongings in preparation to disembark, eager to get off the boat after the overnight journey across the Irish Sea. Among them was a tall man with lank, rat-tail black hair that blew across his face in the wind billowing off the Mersey. He wore a nondescript overcoat and carried a single, long duffle bag, black canvas with brown leather accents and handles. As the ferry docked at the terminal, the man joined the queue of passengers preparing to disembark. He stood calmly, one hand holding his ticket, the other firmly grasping the duffle bag. Its size and shape did not draw any particular attention. Around him, families fussed over-excitable children while solo travellers checked documents and travel plans. Nobody paid the man any mind.

When it was his turn, the man nodded and presented his ticket to the agent. He then proceeded down the ramp to the terminal. The bag swung heavily at his side, its contents making no sound.

'Just the one bag, sir? ' the agent asked as the man clomped down the wooden ramp.

'Aye, a bit of a fishing holiday, sure,' replied the man, not bothering to meet the agent's eye.

Stepping onto the quay, the man glanced around briefly before heading towards the exit gates. He moved with purpose but without haste, a man on a schedule but not rushed. Within moments, he had passed through the terminal and disappeared into the bustling streets of Liverpool, just one more arrival fading into the flow of traffic.

The man walked briskly along Cleveland Street, weaving through the crowds going about their daily business. The docks always meant crowds, men looking for work, sailors just off the boats and stevedores hauling cargo to and fro. He moved with purpose, eyes focused straight ahead, drawing little attention beyond the occasional sideways glance at the large canvas duffle bag swinging at his side. He turned right at the corner of Argyle Street, heading inland and putting distance between himself and the waterfront. The crowds thinned out, replaced by office workers and the occasional well-dressed lady out for a morning stroll. He passed redbrick shopfronts and neat row houses, everything tidy and orderly.

Up ahead, the striking facade of Birkenhead Central Station came into view. The man quickened his pace slightly, checking his watch, eager to catch the next available train. He requested a single to London Paddington at the ticket counter, paying in cash from a roll of notes pulled from his coat pocket. Ticket in hand, he made for the southbound platforms. A British Railways, Western Region train was preparing for departure, clouds of steam hissing from the engine as it idled at the platform.

The man boarded a second-class carriage and shuffled along the corridor until he found an empty compartment. He closed the door behind him, lowered the blinds, and stowed his bag on the overhead rack. Taking his seat by the window, he removed his coat, draping it on the seat beside him. The train lurched and slowly pulled out of the station. He settled in for the journey, allowing his eyes to drift shut as the locomotive picked up speed, carrying him south towards his destination. The train click-clacked over the rails, rocking gently back and forth. He let the motion soothe him, conserving his energy for what lay ahead. There would be time enough for that when they reached London. For now, he rested, the city fading into the distance behind him as the train sped on through the English countryside.

Malone exited Paddington station into the bustling streets of London. Consulting a pocket map, he oriented himself and walked south towards Lancaster Gate. The pavements were crowded with businessmen in suits, ladies out shopping, and the occasional vagrant slumped in a doorway. He drew little notice, just another face in the urban hive. After several blocks, he turned down a side street and approached a grubby-looking establishment bearing a creaking sign that read 'Paddington Lodge - Rooms to Let'. Pushing through the door revealed a dimly lit interior smelling of lousy cooking and cigarette smoke. He walked up to the counter where a bored-looking clerk sat reading a racing form.

'I need a room for the night,' Malone said brusquely, sliding a five pound note across the counter. The clerk glanced up, took in Malone's rough appearance, and pocketed the cash without comment. He slid a key attached to a large wooden tag across the counter.

'Top of the stairs, last door on the left. Pub's two doors down if you want a pint.'

Malone nodded, took the key, and headed for the stairs. The room was small and sparse, with peeling wallpaper and a sagging mattress, but it would suffice. He dropped his bag on the floor, removed his coat, and lay down. Sleep did not come easily.

The following day, he woke up late. A splash of lukewarm water from the basin and a quick comb of his hair were enough to make himself presentable. He picked up his duffle bag, went downstairs, threw his key onto the desk and made for the door. Two blocks over he found his meeting place, a dark hole in the wall bearing a faded sign reading 'The White Hart'. Warm air heavy with the odour of meat pies enveloped him as he walked inside. Scanning the few lunchtime patrons, he quickly spotted who he was looking for. In a corner booth sat Liam Dennett. Malone walked over and slid into the opposite seat. Dennett looked up nervously.

'Do you have it?' he asked.

Dennett nodded, reached into his jacket pocket and withdrew a photograph. He slid it across the table. Malone picked it up and examined it briefly before slipping it away. 'Baker's at a holiday park in Caister-on-Sea, in Norfolk. I've written the directions on the back.' Dennett said, his voice low. 'When will it be done?'

Malone fixed Dennett with a cold stare. 'Best you don't know. Many thanks for the information.'

He slid out from the booth and, without another word, walked out of the pub, leaving his untouched beer behind. Dennett watched him go, a mixture of apprehension and relief on his face.

Malone quickly made his way to the Lancaster Gate Underground station. Descending the steps, he bought a ticket, passed through the turnstile, and caught an eastbound train. As the car rumbled through the tunnels towards Liverpool Street Station, he reviewed the photograph and directions, committing the details to memory. His destination was clear. All that remained now was to conclude his business with Thomas Baker. By this time tomorrow, it would be done.

The train from Liverpool Street Station to Caister Camp Halt rumbled along the tracks, the rhythmic clicking of the wheels over the rails lulling Malone into contemplation as he stared out the window. He sat with his long duffle bag across his lap, one hand placed possessively atop it. Across the aisle an elderly woman gave him periodic sidelong glances, no doubt curious about the contents of his bulky luggage and his ultimate destination. Malone ignored the nosy woman, watching the scenery pass by in a blur of green fields and trees.

Later, the conductor entered the passenger carriage to check everyone's tickets. Malone wordlessly handed over his ticket when prompted. The conductor glanced at the ticket's destination and then did a double take, a flicker of recognition passing across his face. 'Heading up to Caister then?' the conductor inquired in a friendly tone, making conversation. Malone simply nodded in reply. 'Wrong season for pike fishing, isn't it?' The conductor looked pointedly at Malone's bag, clearly suspicious of its contents.

Malone forced a thin smile. 'Can't wait to get started. I fancy me chances this year.'

ALWAYS EAT WHEN YOU ARE HUNGRY

The conductor nodded slowly, clearly unconvinced by Malone's fishing story. 'Right you are then. That bag looks heavy; would you like me to stow it in the guard's van for you?'

Malone's grip on the bag tightened almost imperceptibly at the suggestion. 'No thank you, I'll keep it with me.'

The conductor held up his hands placatingly, backing off. 'No problem sir, just thought I'd offer.' His eyes darted down to the mysterious bag once more before he made to continue down the carriage.

Malone made a split-second decision and spoke up. 'Actually, since you're here, maybe you could help me with something. I'm looking for an old friend of mine but I seem to have lost his address somewhere along the way. I've got a photograph of him with his family; perhaps you'll recognise him?'

Malone withdrew the telling photograph from his pocket and held it up for the conductor to see. The conductor glanced at it briefly, froze for a moment as recognition set in, then quickly schooled his features back to neutrality. 'Can't say I recognise them, Sir. But good luck finding your friend.' Touching the brim of his hat, the conductor swiftly moved down the carriage, leaving Malone to replace the photograph in his pocket, his eyes calculating his next move.

The train slowly pulled into Caister Camp Halt station, the brakes squealing as it stopped at the small rural terminus. Stepping onto the platform, Malone paused to get his bearings, scanning the mostly empty station surroundings.

Off to one side, the conductor busied himself unloading luggage from the guard's van. As Malone walked past with his bag slung over one shoulder, the conductor's eyes were drawn to the loose zipper along the side. Through the gap, the unmistakable wooden stock of a rifle was visible, poking out from beneath rumpled clothing. The conductor froze for a moment, stunned by the sight. As Malone strode along the platform, the conductor overheard him ask a station staff member for directions to Caister Holiday Park.

The conductor abandoned his unloading duties and tailed the stranger at a distance until he left the concourse, at which point he darted into the station office and made a beeline for the telephone. He quickly rang Caister police station, cupping his hand over the mouthpiece as he spoke in hushed tones.

'Inspector Collins? Hi, it's Johnnie at Caister Camp Halt. Yeah, hello. I thought I'd give you a ring. A passenger just got off the Liverpool Street train carrying some sort of firearm in a long bag. Looked like a rifle to me. He's a rough-looking bloke with an Irish accent and long, dark hair. The thing is, he showed me a photo of a young couple I remember from earlier in the season. Lovely people with a newborn. They were going to stay with a relative if I remember rightly. Something about convalescing. Anyway, sounded like he might be looking for them?'

Finishing his call, Johnnie, the conductor, bid his farewell to Collins and replaced the handset on the wall phone with a ding. *'Dunno what this place is coming to, I really don't. Nice quiet little backwater in the middle of nowhere. First, the Yanks, then the Italians, and now the Irish are here. Dear-oh-dear, what the bloody hell is going on?'*

Chapter 22

The Calm Before The Storm

The holiday park at Caister-on-Sea buzzed with cheerful activity on a sunny summer day on the Norfolk coastline. Children laughed and squealed with delight as they played on the swings, slides, and merry-go-rounds in the playground area. Inside the sports room, a group of men gathered around the sixpenny bagatelle gaming machines, cigarettes dangling casually from their mouths as they concentrated intently on aiming the miniature metal ball bearings into the scoring cups. Young couples pedalled four-wheeled bicycles built for two along the neat gravel pathways, the girls' colourful floral dresses and petticoats fluttering lightly in the gentle sea breeze.

From the main dining hall, strains of the lively camp song 'Always Eat When You Are Hungry' drifted out the open windows as the lunch service began, the clinking of plates and utensils mixing with the melody. The smell of freshly fried fish and chips wafted in the air, making stomachs rumble and mouths water in anticipation. On the sandy beach, paddlers emerged from the wooden beach huts and strolled across the pebbly shore towards the water, the women in modest one-piece wool bathing costumes, the men in shorts or trousers rolled up to the knees. A lively football game got underway on the beach, with players using knotted handkerchiefs to hold back their wind-tousled hair as they darted up and down the makeshift pitch. Multi-coloured rubber beach balls bounced between laughing children playing catch near the shoreline. Nearby, babies and toddlers splashed happily under the watchful eyes of their mothers in the shallow concrete paddling pool, protected from the waves. The larger swimming pool was filled with people of all ages enjoying a refreshing dip, floral and polka dot swimming caps dotted across the clear blue surface like colourful lily pads. On the putting green, children swung miniature golf clubs awkwardly as they attempted to sink their balls into the holes, concentration furrowing their brows beneath their sunhats.

And so it came to be that Constable Jim Jordan and his undercover team arrived in their nondescript grey Fordson E83W van and parked alongside the other traders' vehicles in the car park behind the catering block. Jordan jumped out and wandered up to the back door, knocking on it firmly and with authority. The sounds of clanging pots and sizzling fat momentarily grew louder as it swung open. Before him stood a rotund cook, his white uniform stained with grease and flour.

'Buongiorno, come posso aiutarti?' the cook asked in Italian, eyeing Jordan curiously.

Jordan cleared his throat. 'Good morning. I'm here to see Mr. Lillo Rossi about some work that needs doing,' he replied.

The cook's eyes narrowed slightly, but he stepped aside and gestured for Jordan to enter. 'Un momento, per favore,' he said before turning and shouting something in rapid Italian toward the interior kitchen. Jordan waited inside the doorway, peering down the narrow corridor with shelves stacked high with cans and boxes. The air was thick with the mingling aromas of onions, garlic, and simmering tomato sauce. A teenage kitchen worker emerged from the back, wiping his hands on a dish towel. He nodded silently to Jordan before disappearing through double doors leading to the dining hall. Moments later, the doors swung open again and Lillo Rossi strode into view. His crisp white shirt and black trousers were pristine, in stark contrast to the dishevelled cook. Lillo's dark eyes flashed with curiosity and caution as he approached Jordan. 'You asked for me?' Lillo said in accented English. 'I am Lillo Rossi, the manager here.'

The constable extended his hand in greeting, then leaned toward Lillo and whispered. 'Constable Jim Jordan, Special Branch. A pleasure to make your acquaintance.'

Lillo briskly shook his hand, appraising him. 'Ah yes, likewise. I was told you were on your way.' Lillo nodded almost imperceptibly toward the cook.

'I need to discuss something rather sensitive with you, Mr. Rossi,' offered Jordan, aware of the pretence. 'Is there somewhere private where we could talk?'

Lillo looked back at the cook and barked at him. 'Torna al tuo lavoro!' Lillo watched the cook wander back to the kitchen before nodding. 'Yes, we can talk in my office. Follow me, constable.' He turned toward a narrow staircase at the corridor's end, signalling for Jordan to join him. Jordan glanced back at the cook, who continued to eyeball the pair over his shoulder. Jordan gave a polite nod before following Lillo up the creaking wooden steps.

Lillo closed the office door behind them and gestured to a wooden chair across from his desk. 'Please, take a seat, constable,' he offered as he walked around and settled into the worn leather chair behind the desk. Jordan sat down, glancing around the cramped space crowded with filing cabinets, bookshelves, and stacks of paperwork. 'So then, you mentioned a sensitive matter to discuss?' Lillo prompted, lacing his fingers together on top of the desk.

Jordan leaned forward, dropping the pretence. 'I'm afraid Mr Baker's identity and location here have been compromised. A man matching the description of the one I hear has been lurking about was spotted at a pub in London meeting with Liam Dennett two nights ago.'

Lillo's expression darkened. 'I feared as much when that photograph went missing. The man in the tweed suit must have gotten what he needed from it.'

'It seems likely whoever he's working for has passed the information on to the Dennetts,' Jordan agreed. 'Inspector Bellinger is convinced they'll be sending someone here to seek retribution against Mr Baker.'

'And we both know the Dennetts don't mess around,' Lillo said grimly, rubbing his chin. 'If they've got Tommy's location, we must get him and his family somewhere safe. I've already housed them in the annex to my place with two of my most trusted men keeping watch. But it may not be secure enough if the Dennetts have dispatched one of their professional assassins.'

Jordan nodded. 'I've got a team assembled to assist with their evacuation. We'll get them safely out of Norfolk while we figure out our next move.'

The conversation was interrupted by a knock on Lillo's office door. He glanced at Jordan before calling out, 'Come in.'

The door opened, and Carla, one of the local kitchen staff, poked her head in. 'Sorry to interrupt Mr Lillo, but there's a copper out front asking to speak with you.'

Lillo and Jordan exchanged glances. Lillo tensed, his mind racing through possibilities. 'Did he give his name or say what he wanted?'

Carla shook her head apologetically. 'No, Mr Lillo, just that it was urgent police business, and he needed to talk to whoever was in charge straight away.'

'Right. Thank you, Carla. I'll be out momentarily to deal with this.' Lillo waited until the door clicked shut before turning to Jordan with a grim expression.

Jordan rose from his seat, his hand drifting near his concealed firearm. 'This could be trouble. If word's reached the local police already, we may have a leak, or they're closer than we realised.'

Lillo stood, reaching for a heavy torch sitting on a shelf. 'Best we check this out carefully. This guy may not be a police officer at all. Follow my lead and keep your guard up.'

The two men exited the office and moved briskly through the hallway leading to the main entrance. Lillo kept the torch low but handy, muscles tense. Jordan trailed close behind, eyes scanning their surroundings.

Lillo and Jordan came to the front door to see a uniformed police officer standing nonchalantly on the front step. The officer turned as they arrived, giving a courteous nod. 'Afternoon gents. Are one of you the manager of this establishment?'

Lillo lowered the flashlight slightly, still puzzled. 'Yes, I'm Mr. Rossi. How can I help you officer?'

The policeman pulled out a notepad, flipping it open. 'Right, apologies for the intrusion. I'm Inspector Collins, the Station House Office at Caister Police Station. Um, well, technically, Sub-Inspector, but Inspector does the job just fine. Just following up on a report we received earlier today regarding a suspicious individual seen in the area...' The officer pushed his spectacles back from the end of his nose, looked up from his notebook and gawped, open-mouthed at the pair.

Lillo relaxed his grip on the torch, exchanging a discreet look with Jordan, with the hint of a smile and eyebrows raised. Seemed they could rule out this character being connected to the Dennetts after all. Still, they would need to tread carefully in their response. Lillo focused back on the policeman with a friendly smile. 'Of course, let's discuss this further inside...'

The three men walked purposefully back to Lillo's workplace. The officer removed his cap as he entered the cramped office. 'Again, gents, apologies for the intrusion, but we've had reports of suspicious activity around the camp. Wanted to ask if you've noticed any unfamiliar faces lurking about.'

Collins held up his notebook, pencil at the ready. Lillo shook his head. 'No, can't say that I have. We do get all sorts passing through here though. Holidaymakers are always coming and going.'

'Hmm, alright then,' Collins murmured, jotting something down. 'Though this fellow doesn't quite seem the holidaying type. Described as a rough-looking character. Earlier today, he was spotted leaving the train platform with some rather ominous luggage. Just want to be sure he's not up to any trouble here at the camp.'

Jordan spoke up. 'Did the report mention what was in the luggage that seemed so troubling?'

Collins rechecked his notes. 'Ah yes, the fellow said it looked to be a long, thin bag of some sort with a rifle butt poking out. So naturally cause for concern.'

Lillo and Jordan exchanged a subtle but meaningful look. It seemed their fears were coming to fruition.

'Well then, we certainly appreciate you looking into this,' Lillo said smoothly. 'Do let us know if you require any further assistance. We'll notify you immediately if we notice anyone matching that description lurking around.'

Collins tucked his notebook away. 'Very good. That's all for now gentlemen. Good day to you both.' Collins departed with an efficient nod and doffed his cap. Lillo waited several moments before turning to Jordan, features etched with worry.

'This changes things. We need to get the Bakers to safety immediately. I fear the Dennetts' enforcer has arrived after all.'

Chapter 23

The Confrontation

The early morning bus lumbered down the seaside road, wheels sloshing through puddles left by the earlier rainstorm. As it approached the entrance to Caister Holiday Park, the brakes engaged with a high-pitched squeal, and the bus shuddered to a halt at the regulation stop. The doors folded open with a mechanical clang, and a tall, slender man with dark shoulder-length hair stepped out onto the curb.

Malone paused, collar turned up against the wind. Hefting a long duffle bag over one shoulder, he set off down the path into the holiday park. His boots splashed through murky puddles as he made his way past neatly trimmed hedges and flower beds. In the distance, the sounds of children braving the cold, laughing and splashing in the surf, could be heard between the distant rumblings of thunder. He slowed his pace and scanned his surroundings as he drew nearer to the main concourse. His eyes took in families walking with beach gear and couples strolling hand in hand. With a subtle shift of his bag, he changed course and slipped down a side path leading away from the crowds. His leather jerkin creaked beneath his overcoat as he wound between maintenance sheds and utility buildings, clearly focused on avoiding detection.

Pausing by the cover of a large propane tank, Malone withdrew a crumpled photograph from his pocket. He studied it briefly before folding it away and continuing on. As he moved, one hand drifted casually towards his jerkin pocket, fingers brushing against the steel barrel of a handgun. His eyes remained alert, watching for any signs of employees or holidaymakers as he stealthily made his way deeper into the holiday park grounds and headed for the dining hall. Seeing several families waiting by the main door, hoping for an early start to breakfast, he circumnavigated the entrance and made his way around to the sea-view end of the hall. Peering through the salty, sand-encrusted window he spotted a young girl working on the tables and place settings.

Malone squinted through the shade of his hand and tapped on the pane. 'Can ye open up an' let us in child? It's feckin' freezing out here.' The girl raised her hand to her face at the shock of seeing him. She pointed to the wall clock. 'Non, non signore, too soon, too soon. You come back eight thirty. Breakfast ready then.'

'I'm not here for a feed child, I have messages to conduct. Open the door please. This is not a social call.'

'Non, non signore. No key, no key.'

'Well, go and get the key then, child. I'm getting feckin' blown away out here, aye.'

Francesca backed away from the window pointing to the kitchen doors. 'I get boss.'

'You do that, child'.

Malone made his way around to the main door, ignoring the early birds' stares. A key rattled in the lock as he approached, and the door swung open. A portly cook eyed the stranger with suspicion. 'Si signore. What can I do for you?'

'You can let me in out of this feckin' wind for starters.' He shoved the cook aside, dropped his bag to the floor and tore off his overcoat shaking it with a fury. He threw it on a dining table knocking a flower vase to the floor, smashing it to pieces.

'Che palle!' cried the cook hands held above his head. 'Look, signore, look what you do.'

Malone grabbed the cook by his lapel and frog-marched him to the centre of the dining room, away from the prying eyes of the early birds. 'Never mind the feckin' vase. I'm here for one thing only. I'm going to ask you a simple question. How the rest of your day pans out will depend on the answer ya give. D'youse understand me mister?'

The cook nodded. 'Si signore.'

Malone reached into his pocket and produced a crumpled photograph, holding it in front of the cook's face. The man's eyes narrowed. 'I'm looking for someone who I was told works here. Name of Tommy Baker. Where do I find Tommy Baker?'

The cook paled as the inherent threat radiating from Malone sunk in. He slowly shook his head, wiping his hands nervously on his apron. 'Scusa signore, I no hear nobody this name. We no one called Tommy Baker work here.'

Malone's expression darkened, his patience clearly waning. Before the cook could react, he lashed out and backhanded him hard across the face. The solid blow knocked the portly cook to the floor with a heavy thud. 'I don't take kindly to lies,' he growled at the prone cook. 'You've one more chance to...'

He was interrupted by the return of the young girl rushing into the dining hall. She gasped at the scene before her and immediately called back into the kitchen.

'Signore Rossi!' she cried out urgently. 'Come, come! Come quickly!'

Moments later Lillo burst from the kitchen doors, his gaze taking in the situation between the girl, the cook and the intimidating stranger. His eyes narrowed, immediately sensing the threat. 'What in blazes is going on here?' he demanded of the cook. 'Explain this at once!'

The cook spoke rapidly in Italian as the girl helped him to his feet before frantically scampering back to the kitchen. 'This man, he came asking about some Tommy Baker... I tried to say we've never had anyone here by that name but he refused to believe me, knocked me down. Then Francesca called for you ...'

Lillo's expression was grim as he turned to fully face Malone. 'I believe you have some explaining to do Sir. We don't tolerate abuse of my staff here...'

Malone's eyes flashed dangerously at Lillo's defiant stance. He grabbed Lillo by the collar in a blur of motion and slammed him against the nearest wall. 'Don't be playin' games with me, boyo,' he hissed, his face inches from Lillo's. 'Tell me where Tommy Baker is, or so help me God, I'll paint these walls with your feckin' brains.' Malone slipped a hand inside his jerkin and produced his handgun. He pressed the cold steel barrel firmly under Lillo's chin, causing the man to gasp.

'Now I'm going to ask you one last time,' he said, his voice low and menacing. 'Where...is...Tommy...Baker?'

Lillo met Malone's icy stare unflinchingly despite the gun jammed under his throat. 'You've already been told there is no Tommy Baker here,' he said evenly. 'And, if you don't release me immediately, you'll regret it.'

Malone barked out a harsh laugh. 'Oh I will, will I? And who's going to make me regret it? You and what army?'

At that moment, the kitchen doors burst open with a crash. A multitude of angry kitchen staff poured into the dining hall, brandishing cleavers, rolling pins, and other makeshift weapons. They fanned out in a semi-circle around Malone, shouting angrily in a mix of English and Italian. Malone's eyes widened in surprise as he took in the small army arrayed against him. With a snarl, he released Lillo and took a step back, sweeping his gun back and forth threateningly.

'Back off, the lot of you!' he shouted. But the staff pressed closer, waving their improvised weaponry menacingly. Realising he was outnumbered and outgunned, Malone spat curses under his breath. Keeping his revolver trained on the advancing mob, he scooped up his bag and coat before making a hasty retreat. 'This isn't over!' Malone yelled as he crashed through the front doors in a shower of breaking glass. 'I'll be back to finish this!'

The staff flooded out after him, their faces mixed with anger and determination. But Malone, had already sprinted off into the sprawling holiday park grounds. Just as he disappeared around a corner, the heavens opened up, unleashing a torrent of rain that pelted the ground with a deafening roar. A brilliant flash of lightning illuminated the sky, followed by a thunderous crack that seemed to shake the very earth beneath their feet.

Malone ducked and wove between the colourful chalets and recreational buildings, his breath coming in ragged gasps. His boots squelched in the rapidly forming puddles as he darted from shadow to shadow, his keen ears picking up the telltale sound of approaching police car bells in the distance. The ringing grew louder with each passing second, spurring him to move faster. He clutched his bag tightly to his chest, knowing that failure was not an option for The Dennett Family. Malone vanished into the stormy night, leaving a trail of confusion and unanswered questions.

Jordan and his men arrived on the scene, alerted by the sound of the approaching police cars. As they convened at the dining hall, the ringing grew louder. Moments later, two police cars came screeching into view, skidding to a halt nearby.

Jordan quickly assembled his team. 'Right, lads, let's see what's what here,' he said briskly, leading them towards the chaotic dining hall. Inside, they found Lillo Rossi and his kitchen staff in a state of angry excitement. Shouting voices filled the room along with waving arms and shaken fists. Shattered glass littered the floor near the front entrance. Jordan stepped forward authoritatively and addressed the gathering. 'Alright now, let's have some order here!' His commanding voice cut through the din as he raised his police warrant card above his head for all to see. 'I'm Constable James Jordan from Special Branch. What's happened?'

Lillo came forward, rubbing his throat gingerly where the stranger had held a gun to it. He quickly explained the situation with the Irishman's violent questioning about Tommy Baker. Jordan's expression was grim as he digested this news. 'Right then. I need all non-essential personnel to disperse for now. Lillo, gather your people and get them back to work. We'll deal with the local police.'

The staff began filtering back to the kitchen as several uniformed policemen entered, shaking off the rain. Jordan intercepted them efficiently. 'Constable James Jordan, Special Branch,' he introduced himself, once more offering his warrant card. 'My team has jurisdiction here. I need your men to set up a perimeter and assist us with tracking him down.'

The police officers exchanged glances, uncertainty flickering across their faces. They then looked to Inspector Collins, for guidance. Collins adjusted his spectacles and cleared his throat officiously. 'You heard the man, lads,' he said in his reedy voice. 'Constable Jordan is with Special Branch, so he has jurisdiction here. Let's assist him as requested and set up a perimeter around the place.'

The uniformed policemen nodded and blustered around to follow their orders, dispersing into the rain to begin tracking down the mysterious Irishman. Inspector Collins watched them go, then turned back to Jordan. 'My men will provide whatever support you need, Constable,' he said. 'Just say the word if you require anything further.'

As the policemen moved back into the rain, Jordan gathered his men. 'Right, here's the deal. Davis, you and Rogers check the perimeter of the park grounds. Clayton and Watts take the entertainment area. Move quietly and keep an eye out for our Irish friend. If you spot him, take it easy. He's armed. I'll coordinate with Rossi and the local police from here. Now move out swiftly and silently, lads.'

The team dispersed as Jordan turned back to Lillo. 'Now then, why don't you tell me exactly what happened here...'

Malone panicked as he fled the dining hall, the angry shouts and police bells fading behind him as he plunged into the holiday park grounds. He needed to find somewhere to hide, and fast. The recent events replayed in his mind - he had fucked up, and now the law was after him. Spying the sports hall ahead, an idea formed. Malone made for the building, staying low as he slipped beneath the veranda. Working swiftly, he grabbed a section of tarpaulin that had been blown in from the beach and wrapped the duffle bag in it to conceal it. Crawling beneath the decking, Malone wedged the bundle securely between the wooden supports overhead. He couldn't risk being found with a potential murder weapon on him. With the rifle hidden, his next priority was getting away from the area. He couldn't risk being found loitering here. Keeping low, he crept from the veranda and made for a stand of trees nearby. Using them as cover, he steadily worked his way towards the distant dunes edging the beach. He needed to distance himself from the chaotic scene he had left behind.

Soon Malone was slipping and sliding down the dunes, hunkering low amongst the tufts of marram grass. He slowly and carefully began working his way north, following the shoreline. The tumult at the holiday park had faded away, leaving only the steady shush of waves and crying gulls. He was alone now, a fugitive on the run. After nearly half a mile of tense travel, Malone finally distanced himself from the park. Angling off the beach, he crossed a soggy field and regained the coast road. In the distance, he could make out a bus approaching. Malone waved it down urgently, eager to get far away.

The bus rolled to a stop, and the doors hissed open. 'Blimey, you're lucky, mate,' laughed the conductor. 'He don't usually stop for anyone unless they're at a bus stop and, even then, he'll sometimes drive straight past if he don't like the look of them!'

Malone climbed aboard. 'Cheers, mate,' he called out to the driver. 'I've had enough soakings for one day.' As the bus pulled away, the driver glanced back, smiling at Malone.

'*Funny accent*,' thought the driver. '*He's a long way from home then.*'

The holiday park was out of sight now, obscured by hedgerows. Malone didn't know what he would do next, but at least he'd managed to escape for the moment. Settling into a seat, he watched the rainy coastline slide past the grimy window, carrying him away from the chaos behind.

Chapter 24

The Slip

Jordan stood tall and stern in the grand dining hall, keen eyes surveying the chaotic scene unfolding around him. Guests and staff members alike milled about the expansive room in a state of confusion and panic as Collins worked to take statements from rattled witnesses regarding the incident with the mysterious Irishman. It was abundantly clear to Jordan that the Irishman had already managed to flee the premises, but to where exactly? Time was of the essence if they hoped to capture this dangerous fugitive.

'Alright, listen up, everyone,' Jordan announced, taking charge of the tense situation. 'For your own safety I need all guests to please return to your chalets immediately. We believe the armed assailant has left the area but we need to conduct a thorough search of the entire grounds.'

Reluctantly the frightened holidaymakers began shuffling out of the dining hall, whispering anxiously amongst themselves as they went. One by one, Jordan's men reappeared breathlessly in the doorway with worried looks.

'Well? Did you find any sign of him?' Jordan asked intently.

'No Sir, no sign of him at all,' one of the men replied worriedly. 'He could be anywhere by now.'

Jordan nodded, considering their next moves carefully. 'Right then. We need to comb every inch of this place quickly and carefully. This bastard is armed and extremely dangerous. All of you need to keep your wits about you out there.'

The men nodded gravely at his instructions, dispersing swiftly to recommence the search. Time was running out. With their instructions assigned, Jordan's team fanned out, moving steadily through the holiday park acreage. Behind chalets, along hedgerows, under buildings

- no potential hiding spot went unchecked. An hour passed, then two, with no sign of the fugitive. Finally, as dusk began to fall, they returned, weary and frustrated.

'It's no good guv,' sighed Rogers. 'He ain't here. Somehow, the sneaky bastard has given us the slip.'

Jordan frowned. How had this guy evaded them? The holiday park was fenced and gated. There were only so many ways he could have slipped out undetected.

'Keep at it, lads,' Jordan urged. 'He's here somewhere, I know it. We just have to keep looking.'

But as the fruitless search dragged on, eventually, Jordan had to concede defeat. The fugitive had escaped, seemingly into thin air. For now, the Irishman had eluded justice. But Jordan vowed to himself that this wasn't over. Wherever he had gone, he would run him to ground. The enforcer's days were numbered.

Lillo led the group back to his house on the outskirts of the holiday park, the day's events weighing heavily on them all. Inside, the savoury aroma of Sofia's cooking filled the air - she had prepared a simple but hearty pasta meal for them all. As Jordan's men filed into the cosy kitchen, Lillo made introductions. 'This is my wife, Sofia. She is a fantastic cook and has made enough for everyone.' Sofia smiled warmly, her eyes crinkling at the corners. Lillo gestured to two broad-shouldered men sitting at the table nursing glasses of grappa. 'And these are my most trusted men - Carlo and Dom.' The men nodded in greeting. Jordan eyed them appraisingly. He could tell by their bearing that they were ex-military. He felt reassured knowing Lillo had capable men around him.

Lillo gestured towards the doorway as Tommy and Lizzie entered the kitchen, Lizzie cradling baby James in her arms. 'And these three are why we are all here,' said Lillo, a smile breaking across his weathered face. Tommy nodded in greeting at the men gathered around the table. He looked weary but determined, the toll of recent events evident in the dark circles under his eyes. Lizzie held baby James close to her chest, her gaze shyly taking in the unfamiliar faces. 'Please, come in, come in,' Lillo urged, pulling out a chair for Lizzie. She sat down gracefully, adjusting the infant in her arms. 'Now, we all must be hungry after today's events. Eat, eat!' He bustled about, filling plates with pasta and passing them around.

The men made space at the table, a few leaning over to peek at the sleeping baby. Lillo poured glasses of wine for Tommy and Lizzie. 'To new beginnings,' he said, raising his glass. Murmurs of 'Salute!' echoed around the table as they drank. Tommy met Lizzie's eyes and gave her a small, hopeful smile. After so much hardship, perhaps this motley group could provide the fresh start they needed.

Once they had all filled their plates and settled around the table, Jordan brought the conversation to the day's troubling events. 'Right, well, it seems we underestimated our adversary,' he began grimly. 'Somehow, this character has managed to evade capture and is now in the wind. We need to operate under the assumption that he is still pursuing his objective - locating and eliminating Mr. Baker. This means our top priority must be immediately getting Tommy and his family to a secure location.'

Lillo nodded. 'I agree. We cannot risk keeping them here anymore; it's too dangerous now. But where can they go that this guy will not find them?'

The men sat in contemplative silence for a few moments. Finally Lillo spoke up. 'I think I may know a place. Carlo, Dom, do you remember the farmhouse where we stayed with the family after the POW camp was disbanded?' The two men nodded, recalling the kindness shown to them by the farmer who had taken them in. 'Old man Rallison and his family still run the place, I recall. He won't mind helping us out. We can have the Bakers there first thing tomorrow morning.'

Murmurs of assent rippled around the table. It was decided. They would quietly relocate the Baker family and hide them in the secluded farmhouse until the fugitive was captured or called off. They would leave no trail for the ruthless gunman to follow. 'In the meantime, gentlemen, we must take watch throughout the night in shifts in case our Irish friend decides to show his face,' Lillo continued.

With their plans set, the men finished their meals and prepared to mobilise. The coming night would be long, but it was a necessary effort to protect the lives at stake. As they moved into action, Jordan felt the familiar swell of determination that came with pursuing justice. The fugitive may have escaped today, but his time was running out. Jordan would see to it personally.

As the first rays of the sun crept over the horizon, Constable Jim Jordan stepped into Lillo Rossi's small, cramped office and shut the door behind him. The closing of the door muffled the sounds of activity emanating from the main room of the holiday park building, where the others were busily preparing for the imminent evacuation of the Baker family. Jordan picked up the black Bakelite telephone receiver from its cradle on Lillo's cluttered desk and dialled the direct line to Detective Inspector Ronald Bellinger's office.

'Bellinger,' came the businesslike voice on the other end of the line after just two rings.

'It's Jordan, Sir,' the constable responded briskly, forgoing any pleasantries. 'I'm calling with an update on the situation here in Caister-on-Sea regarding the Baker family.'

Jordan then proceeded to provide a detailed account of the previous day's dramatic events - the tense confrontation in the dining hall with the armed Irishman, his subsequent escape into thin air, and the group's unanimous decision to immediately relocate Tommy, Lizzie and baby James to a more secure location to evade any further attempts on their lives. Bellinger listened attentively without interruption, absorbing the new information and assembling an updated mental picture of the evolving situation. When Jordan finished briefing him, the Detective Inspector spoke up in his usual authoritative manner.

'This character you described matches the profile of an IRA enforcer MI5 have been keen to apprehend for some time now.' Bellinger stated. 'He goes by the name of Malone, and he's wanted for gun running, extortion, and suspected involvement in several unsolved murders back in Ireland. If we can capture him, it would be a major coup for British Intelligence in combating the IRA threat.'

Jordan nodded in understanding. 'I understand completely, Sir. My team here is prepared to pursue this Malone with everything we've got. However, our foremost priority is getting the Baker family to safety before Malone has another chance to find them.'

'Yes, that's the wise move here,' Bellinger agreed. 'Leave no trail or indication for Malone to be able to follow you and the Bakers. Keep me closely informed of any new developments as they occur. I'll make sure our intelligence sources are listening out for any chatter or information on Malone's current whereabouts.'

'Of course, Sir. You have my word on that,' Jordan promptly replied.

'Good man,' Bellinger responded approvingly. 'We'll get this murderous bastard, Jordan. His days of evading justice and bringing harm to innocents are numbered; you can be sure of that.'

Jordan felt a swell of determination rising at his superior's steadfast words. 'I'll make certain of it personally, Sir. You have my word on that.'

The two men exchanged more details and specifics regarding coordination and the next steps. Then Jordan rang off the call, dropping the receiver back on its hook. Now, it was time to turn his entire focus onto the critical task at hand—safely relocating Tommy, Lizzie, and baby James into hiding before Malone could make another lethal move against them.

Jordan exited Lillo's office and rejoined his team in the main room. The men were bustling about, carefully packing Tommy and Lizzie's belongings into the grey Fordson van parked outside. The air was thick with tension, and the muffled sounds of hurried footsteps and hushed conversations filled the space.

'Alright, lads,' Jordan called out, his voice cutting through the commotion. 'We're moving the Bakers to old man Rallison's farmhouse. Take Lillo and follow his directions to the letter. We can't afford any mistakes, not with this Malone character still out there.' His eyes scanned the room, meeting each man's gaze to drive home the seriousness of the situation. The team nodded in understanding, their faces set with determination. They knew the gravity of the situation and the importance of their task. Each man silently vowed to do whatever it took to keep the young family safe.

Lillo approached Jordan, his brow furrowed with concern, worry lines etched deep into his weathered face. 'I've spoken with old man Rallison. He's expecting us and will have everything ready. The old barn's been converted into a cosy living space – it should keep them comfortable and out of sight.'

Jordan clapped Lillo on the shoulder, a gesture of both gratitude and camaraderie. 'Good man. We appreciate all you've done.'

Lillo then turned to Dom and Carlo, who stood nearby, ready for action. 'You two, I need you to stay here at the house. Sofia needs protection, and I trust you both with her safety. Keep your eyes peeled for anything suspicious.'

Dom and Carlo exchanged glances before nodding in agreement, a silent understanding passing between the two ex-soldiers. 'Of course, Lillo,' Dom confirmed, his voice low and steady. 'We'll guard her with our lives. No harm will come to Sofia while we're here.'

As the last of the bags were loaded into the van, Jordan did a final sweep of the area, his trained eyes searching for any signs of trouble or surveillance. Satisfied that everything was in order, he motioned for Tommy and Lizzie, who stood nervously to the side with baby James bundled tightly in Lizzie's arms. The young couple looked pale and frightened, the weight of their situation evident in their tense postures.

'It's time,' Jordan said softly, his tone gentler now as he addressed the small family. 'Let's get you to safety. We'll have you settled at Rallison's farm before you know it.'

Chapter 25

The Returning

Malone returned to the camp late at night, the faint sound of music and laughter drifting on the sea breeze. He moved stealthily through the shadows, his footsteps barely audible on the soft sand. The Irishman's eyes, keen and alert, scanned the darkened surroundings for any sign of movement. Satisfied that he was alone, he crouched low and reached under the veranda of the sports hall, his fingers finding the familiar contours of his hidden duffle bag. Removing the rifle from its incarceration, the cold metal felt reassuring in his hands as he checked the sights and magazine. Satisfied with his inspection, Malone slung the weapon over his shoulder, its weight a grim reminder of the task ahead. The assassin from Enniskillen adjusted his stance, ready to melt back into the night and carry out the Dennett Family's deadly commission.

Making his way to a secluded corner of the grounds, Malone took position behind a weather station near the wooden steps leading down to the beach. Here he would have a clear line of sight if needed but remain hidden in darkness. He checked his watch - 10:45 pm. The dance would go on until 11:00 pm, giving him time to prepare. Malone stared at the calm sea as he waited, breathing slowly and steadily. The dancehall loudspeakers crackled to life and a cheerful voice announced the last waltz of the evening. Strains of 'The Tennessee Waltz' drifted through the air, followed by enthusiastic applause as the music ended.

The announcer's voice returned, inviting everyone to join in for 'Goodnight Irene' - the traditional camp singalong to end each night. Malone tensed, gripping his rifle tightly. This was the moment the assassin had been waiting for.

As the 'Goodnight Irene' chorus sounded, holidaymakers began spilling noisily out of the dance hall, heading back to their lodgings in scattered groups. Their cheerful, somewhat boozy voices rang out in the night air, singing the refrain. Malone tracked them with his eyes, breathing steadily. A family of five passed near him, the parents swinging their sleepy young children between them as they sang together. Malone's finger rested lightly on the trigger. He watched them fade into the darkness, heading down the path towards the chalets. More revellers emerged, their song and laughter covering any slight sounds of Malone's movements. The song ended, the campers' voices rising passionately for the final verse. Malone's eyes narrowed, focusing intently on the doorway. He slowed his breathing further, body coiled and ready. The song ended with resounding applause and cheers from the campers, their voices echoing through the night air. In the sudden burst of activity, the assassin prepared to act. Malone's keen eyes scanned the area, searching for his target amidst the celebratory chaos. The Irishman's breathing remained steady, his finger ghosting over the trigger as he waited for any sign of his quarry.

The exterior camp lights winked out one by one, enveloping the grounds in darkness. An eerie silence descended, broken only by the waves crashing on the sands and the rhythmic whir of the weather station's wind monitor overhead. The assassin reached into his pocket, retrieving a folded campsite map. Unfolding it carefully, he held it up to catch the moonlight. A wispy cloud drifted across the moon, and Malone quickly struck a match, its sharp sulphur scent mingling with the briny sea air. Cupping the fragile flame, he scanned the map, searching for Beach Boulevard. There - near the top, running parallel to the shoreline. Malone's eyes tracked down the boulevard, finger trailing over the small numbered chalets until he found it: Number 234. He noted its location, then shook the match out just as it singed his fingertips. Malone folded the map and returned it to his pocket, wincing slightly at the mild burn. Peering through the darkness, he could just make out the silhouette of Beach Boulevard's chalets. Malone slung his rifle over his shoulder and moved silently from behind the weather station, down the access steps and towards the moonlit beach. He kept to the shoreline as he walked along the water's edge, the foaming surf masking his footsteps.

He reached the far end of the beach undetected. Crouching low, he scanned the tidy rows of chalets. Somewhere among them was his mark - Baker. Malone would find him tonight. Gripping his rifle, he abandoned the beach, carefully tiptoeing up the wooden access stairs. Somewhere in the darkness, a nightjar called, its strange, repetitive churring rising and falling. Malone froze, listening intently, his senses strained for any other sound - the scuttle of a mouse or the whisper of bat wings. But the night was still once more. Once on the grass, he wiped the sand from his boots, carefully removing all traces for fear of leaving footprints. He slowly walked along the boulevard, counting the chalet numbers - 229, 230 - until he found 234. Standing outside the door, he checked neighbouring chalets. In the distance, he could see one or two chalet lights were still on, but everything was silent around him. Checking, he emerged from the shadows to face the door. He gave the door an almighty kick, and the lock burst away from the wood surround. Gripping his rifle, Malone charged inside the dark chalet.

The night air was shattered by a sudden burst of gunfire, the sharp cracks echoing down the rows of darkened chalets. Inside their tiny homes, holidaymakers were startled from their sleep. Wives gasped and pulled bed sheets up in fright as husbands scrambled to find trousers or don dressing gowns.

In number 231 Arthur Gibbs sat bolt upright in bed. 'What in blazes?!' he shouted, fumbling for his spectacles. His wife Gladys clutched their young son.

'Arthur, what is it? What's happening?' she whispered through trembling lips. Arthur shook his head, straining to see through the window.

All along Beach Boulevard, doors creaked open cautiously. Men in various states of undress peered out into the night, seeking the source of the disturbance. Mothers soothed crying children. A baby wailed from 235.

In 237, newlyweds Edward and Eileen O'Leary crouched on the floor. Edward crawled to the door and slowly cracked it open. His eyes went wide. 'My God, Eileen, stay down!'

Holidaymakers exchanged fearful, confused glances up and down the row of chalets. Husbands motioned for wives and kids to stay put. Some men crept outside barefoot, gathering in small groups as they stared towards the dark end of the boulevard. Nervous muttering rippled through the crowd. What had happened? Was someone hurt? Should they call for help?

Before anyone could act, a man's anguished cry filled the night air followed by another shot, echoing across the quiet campground. The holidaymakers froze, exchanging horrified looks. Some pulled their loved ones closer while others craned their necks to see what was happening. Down the row, a child's frightened wail rose up once more. Mothers soothed their children, speaking in hushed, worried tones. Fathers and husbands stood poised in doorways, unsure whether to go outside. The air was thick with tension as the echoes of the gunshot faded, leaving an uneasy silence hanging over the camp.

Malone burst into the darkened chalet, rifle poised to fire. His eyes rapidly scanned the small, sparsely furnished room before settling on the rumpled bed in the corner. Without hesitation, he aimed and fired repeatedly, sending bullets tearing through the thin mattress in a deafening cacophony that echoed off the bare walls. Feathers exploded into the air as the pillows were shredded by gunfire. Breathing heavily, he flicked on the light and surveyed the carnage. Bullet holes riddled the once crisp white sheets and blankets. Feathers spilled from the ravaged pillows, drifting in the gloom and settling on the worn wooden floor. The seaside chalet was utterly empty, devoid of occupants. Tommy Baker was nowhere to be found. With a cry of rage, the Malone fired again in anger, the remaining round reverberating in the small space. His quarry had somehow eluded him. Tommy Baker was gone.

Voices outside made the Irishman snap to attention. The gunshots had drawn the notice of others. He hastily killed the light and moved to the back of the small cabin, mind racing as he formulated his escape. In one angry motion, he kicked through the wooden window slats smashing the remaining broken panes with the butt of his rifle and climbed outside into the cool night air. Reaching into his coat, he retrieved his box of matches. The Irishman ignited the contents with a light from one of the matches. The box burst into flames. He tossed it back through the shattered window and onto the bed. As the fire took hold, greedily consuming the dry mattress material, Malone slipped into the darkness. Moving swiftly down the creaky wooden steps, he disappeared onto the moonlit beach just as the holidaymakers finally emerged from their chalets to investigate the commotion.

The night warden's footsteps echoed softly on the gravel path as he made his rounds, his flashlight sweeping across the darkened cabins and silent caravans. The peaceful calm of the holiday park, usually filled with the laughter of families and the chatter of vacationers, was suddenly shattered by the sharp crack of gunfire. He froze in his tracks, heart pounding against his ribs, straining his ears to pinpoint the source of the disturbance. Another shot rang out, the sound reverberating through the still night air, followed by muffled shouts and the distant crash of breaking glass.

'Bloody hell,' he muttered, jogging towards the disturbance.

An eerie orange glow caught his eye as he rounded the corner onto Beach Boulevard. Smoke billowed from one of the chalets, angry flames licking at the wooden walls and reaching hungrily towards the night sky. The acrid scent of burning wood filled the air and carried on a breeze that fanned the growing inferno.

'Christ almighty!' he exclaimed, his voice barely audible over the crackling of the fire.

ALWAYS EAT WHEN YOU ARE HUNGRY

The warden spun on his heel and sprinted back towards the camp offices, lungs burning with each desperate breath. Gravel crunched beneath his feet as he ran, his mind racing about evacuation plans and potential casualties. He burst through the main office door, nearly stumbling in haste, and snatched the phone from its cradle. With trembling fingers, he dialled 999, his heart pounding so loudly he could barely hear the ringtone.

'Emergency services, there's a fire at Caister Holiday Park!' he gasped into the receiver, his words tumbling out in a frantic rush. 'Send help quick! We've got a fully engulfed chalet, and I don't know if anyone is inside. We need fire engines now!'

Slamming down the receiver with a resounding clatter, he dashed back into the night, the cool air hitting his flushed face. Panic gripped him like an icy fist as he raced towards Lillo's house, his feet pounding the gravel path, praying the manager would know what to do in this crisis. He reached the familiar dwelling and pounded on the door with frantic urgency, out of breath and wild-eyed, his chest heaving from exertion.

Sofia answered the door, wrapped in a floral dressing gown, her hair dishevelled from sleep. Her eyes, still heavy with slumber, widened as she took in the sight before her. 'What on earth is happening?' she asked, alarm spreading across her face as she absorbed his disorganised appearance and panicked expression. The cool night air sent a shiver down her spine.

'Fire... gunshots... Beach Boulevard,' he panted, struggling to form coherent sentences as he gulped for air. His hands trembled as he gripped the doorframe for support. 'Where's Lillo? We need him now!' The urgency in his voice was palpable, cutting through the stillness of the night.

Sofia's face paled, her eyes widening with shock and fear. She clutched her dressing gown tighter around her body as if to shield herself from the terrible news. 'He's not here. He left this morning.

He won't be back until tomorrow morning,' she stammered, her voice barely above a whisper. Then, as the gravity of the situation sank in, she asked, 'What do you mean, gunshots? Are people hurt?' Her voice quavered, betraying the terror that was quickly taking hold.

With that, Carlo emerged from the annexe, his stocky frame filling the doorway. His weathered face creased with concern as he took in the scene before him. 'What's all the noise about?' he demanded, his deep voice resonating in the tense atmosphere. His eyes darted between Sofia and the panicked messenger, sensing the gravity of the situation. At a loss for words, the warden shook his head, his mind reeling from the night's events. In the distance, bells began to ring, their ominous pealing cutting through the night air, signalling the approach of emergency vehicles.

Chapter 26

Fire, Fire!

The clanging of bells pierced the night as fire engines roared into the holiday park, a discordant symphony of urgency. Firefighters leapt into action with practised precision, uncoiling hoses and shouting orders as they assessed the inferno engulfing chalet 234. The orange glow of the flames cast eerie shadows across the once-tranquil grounds, transforming the idyllic setting into a scene of chaos and fear.

A burly fire officer's face already streaked with soot corralled the gathering crowd, his voice booming over the crackling flames and the hiss of steam. 'Stand back, folks! For your own safety, please stay well away from the flames!' The spectators reluctantly shuffled backwards, their eyes never leaving the spectacle before them.

Children clung to their parents' legs, wide-eyed and trembling, their small faces a mixture of fear and fascination. Babies wailed in their mothers' arms, startled by the commotion and acrid smoke that stung their eyes and noses. Fathers paced anxiously, their faces etched with worry and anger at the disruption of their peaceful holiday. Some muttered curses under their breath, while others stood stunned, struggling to comprehend the sudden turn of events.

The firefighters worked with practiced efficiency, their movements a well-choreographed dance of urgency and skill. They dragged the heavy supply hose from the Dennis fire pump to the nearby children's paddling pool, now serving as an emergency reservoir, its cheerful blue surround a stark contrast to the hellish scene around it, its contents quickly depleted as water gushed from the pumps, arcing through the air to douse the hungry flames that licked at the night sky. Steam hissed as water met fire, filling the air with a thick, choking mixture of smoke and vapour that swirled and eddied in the flickering light. The acrid stench of burning wood and melted roofing felt assaulted their nostrils, causing people to cough and gag as the noxious fumes invaded their lungs. Desperate to filter the toxic air, holidaymakers covered their faces with whatever they had at hand – damp towels hastily snatched from bathrooms, t-shirts yanked off backs, even pyjama jackets hurriedly rolled up around their heads. The makeshift masks offered little protection against the choking smoke, but it was all they had as they watched their neighbourhood succumb to the fire's relentless attack. Beneath it all lay an undercurrent of fear – the acrid tang of a holiday paradise suddenly turning dangerous, its veneer of safety stripped away in an instant.

As the flames receded under the relentless assault of water, the true extent of the damage became apparent. Chalet 234 stood as a blackened skeleton, its windows shattered and walls scorched beyond recognition. The roof had partially collapsed, revealing the charred remnants of what had once been a cosy vacation home. Miraculously, the neighbouring chalets had escaped with only minor damage, their sides bearing charred streaks as a testament to their close call. The firefighters continued to work, hosing down the smouldering ruins to prevent any resurgence of the blaze. Confused children tugged at their parents' sleeves, asking questions without easy answers. 'Mummy, why is that house burning?' a little girl with pigtails whimpered, her voice barely audible above the commotion. 'Dad, are the bad guys coming to get us?' a young boy asked, his imagination running wild with possibilities. Their innocent queries hung in the air, unanswered amidst the chaos, as parents struggled to find words of comfort that wouldn't ring hollow in the face of such destruction.

Adults exchanged worried glances, their anger at the disruption slowly giving way to a creeping fear that settled in the pit of their stomachs. What had caused this fire? Was it an accident – a carelessly discarded cigarette or a faulty electrical appliance? Or was it something more sinister – an act of arson or sabotage? The holiday park, once a haven of carefree fun and relaxation, now felt exposed and vulnerable under the harsh glare of emergency lights. The sense of security that had drawn families to this coastal retreat had been shattered, leaving a growing unease that threatened to cast a pall over the remaining days of their vacation.

Carmello and Domenico arrived at the fire scene, their faces etched with grim determination as they surveyed the smouldering ruins of Chalet 234. The acrid smell of smoke hung heavy in the air, mingling with the salty breeze from the nearby sea, creating a pungent cocktail that assaulted their senses. They exchanged a knowing glance, their military training kicking in as they assessed the situation.

'This was no accident,' Carlo muttered, his eyes narrowing as he scanned the area, taking in every detail with seasoned scrutiny. 'Tommy and Lizzie's old place was locked up tight. Empty. Not a soul in sight.'

Dom nodded, his jaw clenched, muscles twitching beneath his skin. 'The Irishman. Only he'd be idiot enough to think they'd still be here. He's a fucking amateur, if you ask me.'

'Yeah, and which also means he's probably still out there somewhere,' Carlo added, his voice low and urgent, tinged with anticipation and concern. 'And he's desperate. That makes him dangerous.'

The two men fell silent momentarily, their minds working in tandem as they considered their next move. Their years of military experience had honed their instincts, and now those instincts were screaming that time was of the essence.

'He'd need cover to escape unnoticed,' Dom said, his eyes darting towards the shoreline, where the darkness of night melded with the inky blackness of the sea. 'The beach. It's the perfect escape route.'

Without another word, they sprang into action. Carlo and Dom moved swiftly, their eyes scanning the ground for any sign of the Irishman's passage. It didn't take long before they spotted what they were looking for – sandy footprints in the grass around the wooden steps leading to the beach, a telltale sign of their quarry's hasty retreat.

'Here!' Carlo called out, pointing to the marks with excitement and grim satisfaction. 'Some leading to Beach Boulevard, some away. He's been here alright.'

Dom's eyes lit up with grim determination, a predatory gleam reflecting in their depths. 'He went down to the beach. I'll follow his trail there. He can't have gone far.'

Carlo nodded, turning back towards the main buildings, his mind racing with possibilities. 'I'll check if he doubled back. We'll corner him. He's running out of options.'

With a quick nod of understanding, born from years of working side by side, the two men split up. Dom raced down the wooden stairs, his feet kicking up sand as he hit the beach, the soft ground barely slowing his determined stride. Carlo sprinted back towards the main concourse, his eyes sharp for any sign of their target, every shadow a potential hiding place.

The chase was on, their military training driving them forward with a singular purpose. The cool night air whipped past them as they moved, their breath coming in controlled, measured bursts. The Irishman was out there somewhere, and they were determined to find him before he could cause any more harm. The hunt had begun, and Carlo and Dom were in their element, their service in the Italian special forces 102nd Swimmers company coming to the fore as they pursued their prey through the darkness.

The grey Fordson van rumbled down the dirt road, kicking up billowing dust clouds as they approached old man Rallison's farm. Jordan and his men and Lillo emerged from the vehicle, their faces a mixture of relief and wariness. The farmhouse stood before them, weathered but sturdy, a testament to the resilience of its inhabitants. Its faded red paint and sagging porch spoke of years of harsh winters and scorching summers, yet it remained a beacon of hope in the vast expanse of farmland.

As they approached, the front door swung open with a creak, revealing old man Rallison himself. Despite his advanced years, his eyes still sparkled with life as he caught sight of Lillo. The old farmer's weathered face, etched with lines of laughter and hardship, broke into a wide grin, and he stepped forward with arms outstretched, his worn boots scuffing the dirt.

'Lillo, my boy!' Rallison exclaimed, embracing the Italian warmly. 'It's been too long. You're a sight for sore eyes!'

Lillo returned the embrace, his voice thick with emotion. 'It's good to see you, old friend. The years have been kind to you.'

Rallison's sons emerged from the house, each greeting Lillo with the same affection their father had shown. The reunion was filled with backslaps and hearty handshakes, years of shared history evident in every gesture. The air was filled with laughter and rapid-fire conversations as they caught up on lost time.

As the greetings subsided, Lillo's expression grew sombre, his eyes searching Rallison's face. 'And how is your wife, my friend? Is she well?'

A shadow passed over Rallison's face, his joy dimming visibly. The laughter lines around his eyes deepened into furrows of grief. 'She's gone, Lillo. Tuberculosis took her last winter. The dust from the crops... It was too much for her lungs in the end.' The group fell silent, the weight of loss hanging heavy in the air. Lillo placed a comforting hand on Rallison's shoulder, words unnecessary between old friends. The wind whispered through the nearby wheat fields, a soft, mournful sound that seemed to echo their sorrow.

After a moment, Lillo turned and gestured to Tommy and Lizzie, who stood nervously by the van with baby James. The young couple looked out of place among the weathered farm buildings, their urban clothes a stark contrast to the rural setting. 'These are the friends I told you about. They need a safe place to stay. They've been through a lot.'

Rallison nodded, his hospitality overcoming his grief. His eyes softened as they fell on the baby. 'Of course. We've prepared the old barn for them. It's not much, but it's warm and dry. We've done our best to make it comfortable.'

Tommy and Lizzie were led to the converted barn, their faces a mixture of gratitude and uncertainty. As they settled into their new temporary home, the reality of their situation seemed to hit them anew. The smell of hay and old wood filled their nostrils, a far cry from the seaside air they were used to. Each new location brought a mixture of hope and fear, the constant uprooting taking its toll on their weary spirits. As the sun began to set, painting the sky in hues of orange and purple, Lillo, Jordan, Clayton, and Watts prepared to depart. Davis and Rogers remained behind their presence a silent promise of protection. The departing group climbed into the van, its engine rumbling to life, echoing across the quiet farmyard.

Tommy and Lizzie stood in the barn doorway, watching as the van disappeared down the track, leaving a trail of dust in its wake. The sense of isolation crept over them, a familiar feeling of being cut off from the world they once knew. The vastness of the surrounding fields seemed to close in on them, emphasising their solitude. Yet, as they looked at each other and then down at baby James, nestled safely in Lizzie's arms, a flicker of determination shone in their eyes. They were together, a small family unit against the world, and for now, that had to be enough. The barn door closed behind them, shutting out the encroaching darkness, as they prepared to face whatever challenges the coming days might bring.

Chapter 27

The Fight

Carlo sprinted towards the main reception area, his heart pounding. As he rounded the corner, he skidded to a halt, taking in the chaotic scene before him. The kitchen staff had spilled out onto the lawn, their faces etched with fear and confusion. The air was thick with the acrid smell of smoke, and the clanging of fire engines pierced the night.

'What's happening?' a young kitchen hand called out, her voice trembling.

Carlo raised his hands, gesturing for calm. 'Listen up, everyone!' His voice cut through the panic, commanding attention. 'The situation is under control, but we have a serious problem.'

The crowd fell silent, all eyes fixed on Carlo.

'The fire was no accident,' he continued his tone grave. 'The perpetrator is still at large. I need you all to return to your quarters immediately for your safety and secure the doors.'

A murmur of alarm rippled through the group.

'A fugitive?' someone gasped.

Carlo nodded grimly. 'Yes, and he's dangerous. We can't take any chances. Move quickly and stay together. Lock your doors and windows. Do not open them for anyone you don't recognise.'

The staff exchanged worried glances, the reality of the situation sinking in. Carlo began ushering them towards the staff quarters, his eyes constantly scanning the surroundings for any sign of danger.

'What about our families?' a cook asked, panic rising in his voice.

'We're taking care of everyone,' Carlo assured him. 'The best thing you can do right now is get to safety and stay there until we give the all-clear.'

Dom sprinted down the beach, his feet pounding against the soft sand. As he neared the water's edge, he veered towards the firmer, wet sand, his pace quickening. The sound of waves crashing against the shore mixed with his heavy breathing as he pushed himself forward. The moonlight cast a silvery glow on the beach, illuminating his path. Dom's eyes scanned the shoreline, searching for any sign of movement or disturbance that might indicate the fugitive's passage. After a few minutes of intense running, Dom spotted the familiar wooden steps leading back to the main reception area of the camp. He slowed his pace, approaching the steps with caution. His chest heaved as he caught his breath, adrenaline still coursing through his veins.

Dom ascended the steps silently. He moved with practised stealth, each footfall carefully placed to minimise noise. As he reached the top of the stairs, he crouched low, using the handrail as cover. From his vantage point, Dom surveyed the area. The camp buildings loomed ahead, dark and silent except for one area. His eyes narrowed as he spotted a faint glow from the kitchen windows. The light spilled out onto the grass, creating long shadows that stretched towards the beach. Dom remained still, his senses on high alert. He listened intently for any unusual sounds, but only the distant crash of waves and the faint rustling of leaves in the night breeze reached his ears. The kitchen light drew his attention like a beacon, raising questions about who might be inside at this late hour.

Carlo waved his arms, gesturing urgently to the gathered kitchen staff. 'Everyone, back to your quarters now! Lock your doors and stay inside until further notice.' As the group moved swiftly across the grounds, Carlo noticed a few stragglers hanging back, their curiosity overriding their fear. 'This is not a drill,' he barked, his patience wearing thin. 'Move, now!'

Still shaken from the recent events, the staff hesitated momentarily before slowly dispersing. Their hushed whispers and worried glances betrayed their unease as they shuffled away from the reception area. As the last few workers turned to leave, one of them suddenly stopped and pointed towards the main building. 'Wait, Mr. Carlo! The lights are on in the kitchen. Should they be?'

Carlo's head snapped towards the illuminated windows, his eyes narrowing. He placed a firm hand on the worker's shoulder, gently but insistently pushing him towards the staff quarters. 'Never mind that. Get inside and lock up, just like I said. Go on now.' The worker opened his mouth as if to protest, but Carlo's stern look silenced any further questions. With a nod, the man hurried off to join his colleagues.

Once the last staff had disappeared into their dwellings, Carlo took a deep breath and surveyed his surroundings. The night air was thick with tension, broken only by the distant sound of waves. Carlo moved with practised stealth, his eyes fixed on the lit kitchen windows as he approached the dining hall. Nearing the building, Carlo pressed his back against the cool exterior wall. He inched his way along, pausing at each window to peer inside, searching for any sign of movement or the intruder.

Dom crept towards the rear entrance of the kitchen area, his body low and tense. He weaved between discarded boxes and waste bins, his eyes scanning for any movement. The night air carried the faint scent of rotting food and bleach, starkly contrasting the usual aromas wafting from the bustling kitchen. As he approached the tradesman's entrance, Dom's heart quickened. The heavy padlock that usually secured the door lay on the ground, its shackle bent and twisted. Someone had forced their way in.

Dom hesitated for a moment, weighing his options. With a deep breath, he gently pushed the door open, wincing at the soft creak of its hinges. He slipped inside, immediately dropping into a crouch. The kitchen was eerily quiet, save for the low hum of refrigerators and the occasional drip from a leaky tap. He pressed his back against a cold metal counter, straining his ears for any sound out of place. For several long moments, there was nothing. Then, suddenly, the unmistakable sound of doors opening and closing echoed through the kitchen.

Dom's muscles tensed. He began to move, each step carefully placed to avoid making noise on the tiled floor. He made his way around prep stations and industrial-sized ovens, always keeping low and out of sight. As he neared the cold room, the sound of rustling grew louder. Dom's breath caught in his throat as he peered around the corner into the open doorway of the walk-in refrigerator.

Carlo approached the dining hall with the stealth of a puma. His eyes darted left and right, scanning for any sign of movement in the shadows. The moon cast an eerie glow across the empty tables and chairs, their silhouettes creating a maze of potential hiding spots. He reached the window, his fingers working deftly to unlatch it without a sound. With practised ease, Carlo hoisted himself up and slipped through the opening, softly landing on the polished floor. The dining hall stretched before him, a cavernous space devoid of its usual chatter and clinking cutlery. Carlo's footsteps were muffled as he made his way across the room, his senses on high alert for any unexpected noise or movement. As he neared the far end of the hall, Carlo's gaze fixed on the swing doors leading to the service section. Soft light spilled through the circular windows in each door, casting twin pools of illumination on the floor. The glow seemed out of place in the darkened hall, a beacon that both drew him in and set his nerves on edge. Carlo paused, listening intently. The silence was oppressive, broken only by the faint hum of distant refrigerators. He took a deep breath, steadying himself for what might lie beyond those doors.

With deliberate slowness, Carlo reached out and pressed his palm against one of the swing doors. He applied gentle pressure, intending to open it just enough to peer through. But as the door began to move, a loud, prolonged creak shattered the silence. The sound seemed to echo through the empty hall, impossibly loud in the stillness of the night. Carlo froze, his hand still on the door, as the noise faded. He held his breath, waiting to see if the unexpected sound had alerted anyone – or anything – to his presence.

Dom's breath caught as he peered into the cooler room. A shadowy figure hunched over the shelves, frantically shoving food into his mouth. The man's movements were frantic, almost animalistic, as he tore into packages and devoured their contents.

Suddenly, the loud creak of the service swing door shattered the silence. Dom tensed, his muscles coiled like springs. The eating figure froze mid-bite, his head snapping towards the source of the sound. Time seemed to stand still for a heartbeat. Then, in a blur of motion, the intruder dropped the food he'd been clutching. His hand dove into a long duffle bag at his feet, emerging with a rifle. The weapon came up smoothly, finding its mark with practised ease. Dom's heart hammered in his chest as he watched, paralysed by the unfolding scene.

A deafening crack split the air as the rifle fired. The muzzle flash illuminated the cooler room briefly, throwing harsh shadows across the intruder's face. Dom caught a glimpse of cold, determined eyes before the gloom enveloped the room. The shot's echo reverberated through the kitchen, seeming to shake the very foundations of the building. Dom pressed himself flat against the wall, his mind racing. He knew Carlo had been approaching from the dining hall - had the bullet found its mark? The acrid smell of cordite filled the air, mixing with the lingering scents of food from the cooler. Dom's ears strained for any sound of movement, of life, from beyond the service door.

Carlo's instincts kicked in as the gunshot rang out. He threw himself to the floor, his body moving before his mind could fully process the danger. Rolling swiftly, he sought cover behind a stack of large cooking pots on the nearby shelving unit.

'Come out, or I'll put a bullet through your feckin' head!' Malone's voice echoed through the kitchen, thick with menace.

Another shot cracked through the air, the bullet ricocheting off metal with a piercing clang. Carlo's heart raced as he assessed his options. Spotting a door across the room, he made a desperate dash for it. His fingers fumbled with the handle, yanking and twisting frantically. The door refused to budge, mocking his efforts with its unyielding presence. Panic rose in Carlo's throat as he realised he was trapped.

Slowly, he turned to face his assailant. Malone stood there, rifle trained on Carlo's chest, a cold gleam in his eyes. Carlo raised his hands, palms out, in a gesture of surrender.

'Where's Baker?' Malone snarled, taking a menacing step forward.

Carlo remained silent, his mind racing for a way out of this deadly predicament. Malone's finger tightened on the trigger, his intention clear.

Then, something shifted in Carlo's demeanour. A small smile played at the corners of his mouth as he lowered his hands to his sides. Confusion flashed across Malone's face, his rifle dipping slightly in response to this unexpected reaction.

A blur of motion erupted behind Malone in that split second of hesitation. Dom emerged from the shadows, wielding a cast iron skillet. The heavy pan connected with Malone's skull with a sickening thud. Malone crumpled to the floor, unconscious before he hit the ground. The rifle clattered harmlessly beside him.

Carlo and Dom exchanged a look of relief, their chests heaving from the adrenaline. Without a word, they set to work. Using kitchen twine, they bound Malone's hands and feet tightly. Working quickly and quietly, they manoeuvred the unconscious man into a nearby catering cart. They covered him with tablecloths, disguising their cargo. They wheeled the cart containing the unconscious Malone to a secluded spot behind the maintenance shed. They stood silently for a moment, the weight of their decision hanging heavy in the air.

Carlo broke the silence first. 'What do we do with him?'

Dom's eyes hardened as he looked at the cart. 'We can't let him go. He'll come back for Tommy and his family.'

They exchanged a knowing glance, memories of their time in the Italian Special Forces flooding back. The 102nd Swimmers company had trained them for moments like this – tough decisions in impossible situations.

'Remember Taranto?' Carlo asked, his voice low.

Dom nodded. 'How could I forget? We swam for hours in the darkness, waiting for the right moment to strike.'

'And when we did...' Carlo trailed off.

'We did what was necessary,' Dom finished.

The two men stood straighter, their postures shifting as if they were once again in their military uniforms. Without a word, they raised their right hands in a crisp salute.

'O vinciamo o moriamo,' Carlo said solemnly.

'Either we win, or we die,' Dom translated, his voice barely above a whisper.

Their eyes met a silent understanding passing between them. They had been through too much together to hesitate now. The safety of Tommy, Lizzie, and little James depended on their decision. Carlo took a deep breath. 'We do what we must, old friend.'

Dom nodded grimly. 'For the greater good.'

They turned their attention back to the cart, ready to deal with Malone once and for all. With cautious glances over their shoulders, Carlo and Dom disappeared into the night with their captive.

Chapter 28

Farewell Malone

Malone's eyes fluttered open, his head throbbing with a pain that seemed to pulse in time with the waves around him. The world swayed and tilted, a disorienting dance that made his stomach churn. A cool, salty mist caressed his face, carrying with it the unmistakable scent of the open sea. The rhythmic sound of waves crashing against the hull filled his ears, much louder and more insistent than the gentle lapping he'd heard on the shore.

He tried to move, to gain his bearings, but his body felt as if it were made of lead, his limbs unresponsive and heavy. As his vision slowly cleared, the harsh reality of his situation came into focus. With a growing sense of dread, Malone realised that he was no longer on solid ground. The gentle yet persistent rocking beneath him confirmed his worst fears – he was on a boat, far out at sea, with endless water stretching to the horizon.

Panic rose in his chest, threatening to overwhelm him. The Irishman struggled against his bonds, the rough twine biting into his wrists and ankles. Each movement sent fresh waves of pain through his battered body. The metallic taste of blood filled his mouth. As he fought against his restraints, Malone's mind raced, desperately trying to piece together how he'd ended up in this predicament and, more importantly, how he might escape it.

Dom and Carlo stood at the helm, their backs to him, guiding the vessel through the choppy, slate-grey waters. The salty spray misted their clothing as they navigated the heaving waves. Malone thrashed against his restraints with renewed vigour, his body writhing on the deck as he tried to catch their attention. The rough wood planks scraped against his skin, but he barely noticed the pain. His cries of desperation were muffled by the thick gag wedged between his teeth, rendering his attempts at communication futile.

With desperate determination born of fear and rage, Malone worked his jaw relentlessly, his tongue pushing and probing at the cloth. Slowly, agonisingly, he felt the gag loosen bit by bit. Sweat beaded on his forehead from the effort, mingling with the sea spray that occasionally showered over the boat's sides. Finally, after an eternity, the gag slipped free, falling away from his mouth.

Seizing his chance, Malone unleashed a torrent of threats and insults, his voice hoarse but filled with venom. The words tumbled out in a rush, fuelled by anger and a primal need to assert some control over his dire situation.

'You bastards!' he roared, his Irish brogue thick with emotion. 'I'll kill you both with my bare hands! You've no idea who you're dealing with!'

His words fell on deaf ears. Dom and Carlo remained stoic, focused on their task. As Malone continued his tirade, hurling insults and threats with increasing desperation, a chilling realisation began to dawn on him. His wild eyes darted frantically around the boat before his gaze dropped to his feet, where he saw the heavy anchor chain wrapped tightly around his ankles, secured with a crude wire bond that bit into his flesh. The shore was now nothing more than a distant smudge on the horizon, barely visible in the gathering gloom. A wave of cold, paralysing terror gripped him as the awful truth became clear. This was no interrogation or negotiation. This was his final journey, a one-way trip into the depths of the unforgiving sea.

'Please,' Malone whimpered, his earlier bravado crumbling. His voice, once filled with venom and defiance, now quavered with naked fear. 'I'll do anything. Name your price. Just don't do this. I'm begging you.' The Irishman's composure shattered as he pleaded for his life, all thoughts of vengeance and retribution forgotten in the face of his impending doom.

Dom and Carlo exchanged a look, their faces grim and set with determination. Without uttering a word, they moved in unison towards the trembling Malone. He thrashed wildly, tears streaming down his face as he begged for mercy, his pleas growing increasingly desperate and incoherent. They lifted him effortlessly, his weakened state offering no resistance to their practised grip. With a single, fluid motion, they heaved him over the side of the boat. Malone's scream pierced the night air but was abruptly cut short as he hit the cold, unforgiving water. The weight of the anchor dragged him down relentlessly. The surface grew distant, a shrinking circle of faint moonlight as he sank into the inky depths. Bubbles escaped from his mouth in a final, silent scream as the pressure increased and darkness enveloped him.

Dom watched the ripples fade into the water's calm surface, his voice devoid of emotion as he spoke matter-of-factly. 'If the anchor comes free, the tides will probably carry him to Lowestoft. At which point, there'll be very little of him left to identify. The crabs will have done their work.'

Carlo nodded silently, his expression unreadable in the dim light. Without another word, they turned the boat back towards shore, the engine's low rumble the only sound breaking the eerie silence of the night.

Chapter 29

Return to Base

As the first rays of sunlight painted the sky in hues of pink and gold, Carlo and Dom guided the boat back to the jetty. The gentle lapping of waves against the hull and the distant cries of seagulls broke the early morning silence. They secured the vessel and made their way across the dew-covered grass towards Lillo's house, their footsteps barely audible on the soft ground. The camp was still asleep, an eerie quiet hanging over the rows of chalets and caravans. The air was crisp and cool, carrying the faint scent of salt and seaweed. Carlo and Dom slipped into the kitchen, their movements precise and silent. Dom reached for a bottle of grappa hidden behind some pots while Carlo retrieved two small glasses from a high cupboard. They poured out the clear liquid, the pungent aroma of fermented grapes filling the air.

As they raised their glasses in a wordless toast, their eyes meeting in silent understanding, the sound of tyres crunching on gravel caught their attention. Through the kitchen window, partially obscured by a thin layer of condensation, they saw a nondescript grey van pulling up, its diesel engine rumbling and cutting through the morning stillness. The vehicle came to a halt with a slight jerk, and for a moment, all was quiet again. Then, almost in unison, the doors to the vehicle opened. Lillo and Jordan alighted from the cab, their movements purposeful and alert. Lillo's face bore a grim expression while Jordan's eyes darted around, ever vigilant. As if on cue, the van's rear doors swung open, and Clayton and Watts climbed from the back, their boots hitting the ground with muffled thuds. The four men converged, speaking in hushed tones, their breath visible in the crisp morning air. Carlo and Dom exchanged a knowing glance, their grappa momentarily forgotten as they observed the scene unfolding before them.

Lillo burst through the door, his face a mask of anger and concern, the lines around his eyes deepening with worry. 'Che diavolo state facendo?' he hissed in rapid Italian, his voice low but sharp. 'Why are you drinking at this time of the day? You were supposed to protect Sofia, not waste time getting drunk all night!' His eyes darted between the two men, searching for answers. Carlo and Dom exchanged a glance, their expressions unreadable, maintaining their composure under Lillo's scrutiny. Jordan stepped into the kitchen, his keen eyes taking in the scene. The tension in the room was palpable, and he sensed that something significant had transpired while he was gone.

'What's happened?' Jordan asked, his voice low and measured, the tone of a man accustomed to handling delicate situations. He looked from Carlo to Dom, then back to Lillo, waiting for an explanation. The silence stretched between them, heavy with unspoken words and hidden truths.

Carlo and Dom exchanged a meaningful glance before Carlo cleared his throat, his posture straightening as he prepared to deliver the news. 'Lillo, there's something you need to know,' he began, his voice low and steady, carrying the weight of their nocturnal activities. 'The Irishman, Malone... he's no longer a threat to any of us.'

Dom nodded solemnly, his face etched with grim determination. 'We took care of it, as we've always done when protecting our own. He's at the bottom of the North Seanow, feeding the fishes.'

Lillo's eyes widened in disbelief, darting between the two men and Jordan, his mind racing to process the implications. 'You... what?' he stammered, his usual composure momentarily shattered.

'We did what was necessary to protect Tommy, Lizzie, and the baby,' Carlo explained, his tone firm and unapologetic. 'It was the only way to ensure their safety and end this menace once and for all.'

Jordan maintained his composure as Carlo and Dom related the events of the night. 'I see,' he said, his voice carefully measured, revealing nothing of his inner thoughts.

Dom turned to Jordan, his stance resolute and unwavering. 'We respect your position, Jordan. We know this puts you in a difficult situation. It's up to you how to handle this information, but we trust you'll do what's right.'

Lillo, visibly shaken by the revelation, attempted to regain control of the situation. He asked Carlo and Dom to leave the room, his voice trembling slightly, but they stood their ground, unmoved by his request.

'We're staying,' Dom said firmly, his loyalty to Lillo and their shared cause evident in his tone. 'We're all in this together now, for better or worse. There's no turning back.'

Lillo ran a hand through his hair, his face etched with worry and the weight of responsibility. He turned to Jordan, his voice barely above a whisper, laden with concern. 'What are the consequences? Will they be arrested for murder? Is there any way to protect them?'

Jordan looked at the three men, his gaze steady and unreadable, assessing the situation with the eye of a seasoned law enforcement officer. After a moment of tense silence that seemed to stretch on for an eternity, he spoke, his words carefully chosen. 'It's a sad day when a wanted felon tries to escape in a boat, but the North Sea gets the better of him, especially when he loses his anchor and chain. A very amateur sailor if you ask me, clearly out of his depth in more ways than one.' A hint of a smile and a raised eyebrow emphasised the subtle indication of his decision. 'I'll tell Inspector Collins of this tragic mishap and put out a missing persons report. Sometimes, the sea claims its own, and who are we to argue with nature?'

The tension in the room visibly eased, shoulders relaxing and breaths released as the implications of Jordan's words sank in. A silent understanding passed between the men. Jordan's eyes fell on the bottle of grappa, its presence a reminder of the bonds that tied these men together. He nodded towards it, a faint smile playing at the corners of his mouth. 'I think you'd better get two more glasses if we're going to drink this bottle dry.'

Lillo hesitated for a moment, then nodded, reaching for the glasses. He poured a measure of the solid Italian spirit for Jordan, his hand steadier now as the immediate crisis had passed. As they raised their glasses in a silent toast, the first stirrings of life could be heard from outside. The holiday camp was beginning to wake, oblivious to the drama that had unfolded during the night.

Carlo cleared his throat, his voice low and serious. 'What about Tommy and his family? When can they come back?'

Jordan took a sip of the grappa, savouring the burn as he considered the question. 'We'll need to keep them at the farm for a few more days to be safe. We'll need to make sure there are no loose ends before we bring them back.'

Dom nodded in agreement. 'We'll keep an eye on things here. If anyone comes sniffing around, we'll know about it.'

Lillo looked at his old friends, a mixture of gratitude and concern in his eyes. 'You've taken a great risk for us. I don't know how to thank you.'

Carlo waved off the thanks. 'We're family, Lillo. It's what we do.'

The men finished their drinks in companionable silence as the sun rose higher in the sky, casting long shadows across the kitchen floor. The weight of their actions hung in the air, but so did a sense of resolution. They had protected their own, as they always had, and would continue to do so.

Jordan set down his empty glass with a soft clink and meticulously brushed down his trousers, smoothing out the wrinkles that had formed during their lengthy drive. He glanced at the clock on the wall, noting the early morning hour. 'I'd better get to Caister police station,' he said, his voice tinged with determination and fatigue. 'I need to start working on that missing person's report before the day gets away from us.' He looked at his three companions, taking in their weary expressions and the dark circles under their eyes. 'You three should get some rest,' he advised, his tone softening with concern. 'It's been a long night, and we all need to be sharp for whatever comes next.' Jordan stood up, stretching his stiff muscles, preparing to face the challenges ahead.

As Jordan turned to leave, Lillo called, 'Jordan, thank you. For everything.'

Jordan paused at the door, looking back at the three men. 'Like Carlo said, we're family now. It's what we do.' He nodded once, a gesture of understanding and respect, before stepping out into the brightening day.

At Caister police station, Constable Jordan settled into a quiet corner, his eyes darting around to ensure privacy before he dialled Bellinger's number. The phone rang twice, the tension mounting with each shrill tone before Detective Inspector Bellinger's voice cut through the line.

'Bellinger here,' he barked, his tone as brash as ever.

Jordan took a deep breath, steadying himself for the report he was about to deliver. He recounted the night's events with measured words, his voice remaining level as he described Malone's tragic 'accident' at sea. The constable's fingers tightened around the receiver as he carefully chose each word, aware of the weight they carried. Bellinger listened in silence, the gravity of the situation detectable even through the phone line. When Jordan finished, he let out a long, weary sigh that seemed to carry the burden of the entire case. 'Well, that's one less problem to worry about,' he said, his voice a mixture of relief and resignation.

'What now, Sir?' Jordan asked, eager for direction in the wake of this unexpected turn of events.

'Now?' Bellinger's voice took on a determined edge, steel underlying his words. 'Now we end this once and for all. I'm putting out an arrest warrant for Liam Dennett. The threat's over, and it's time to bring him in. He'll be behind bars before the day is out, mark my words.' There was a pause, pregnant with unspoken implications, then Bellinger continued, his tone now mellowed, 'Get them kids back home. I want to talk to them here, face to face.'

Jordan nodded instinctively. 'Yes, Sir,' he affirmed. After hesitating, he voiced the question that had been gnawing at him since the night's events unfolded. 'What about Brem-Wilson, Sir? How do we handle him?'

Bellinger's response was immediate and unequivocal, his disdain for the man evident in every syllable. 'He can kiss my arse, the pompous, little fucker. As far as I'm concerned, his big fish cannot be found, and we won't lift a finger to help find him. Let him stew in his own juice.'

Jordan hesitated, wrestling with the moral implications of what had transpired. Finally, he voiced the concern that had been nagging at him, his words careful but pointed. 'But what about the fact that he killed Nedser Dennett, Sir? Shouldn't he be held accountable for that? It doesn't sit right, letting the real murderer walk free.'

Bellinger's tone turned grim, a hint of bitterness creeping into his voice. 'MI5 dance to a different tune, Jordan. It's a bloody travesty, but they're immune from arrest for certain illegal activities. It's a mess, a right bloody mess, but that's the way the system works. Sometimes, lad, justice isn't as blind as we'd like it to be.'

Jordan stepped out of the police station and into the crisp morning air, his breath forming small clouds before him. He walked down the lane to the town centre, now bustling with traders, holidaymakers and locals going about their business. He strode over to the town payphone with a sense of urgency, inserted a couple of coins, and dialled Farmer Rallison's number.

After a brief exchange of pleasantries, he asked to speak with Davis and Watson. The line crackled and popped as the phone changed hands, the sound of shuffling feet in the background.

'Davis here,' came the response, the man's voice tinged with a hint of concern. The background noise faded, suggesting Davis had shifted to a quieter position in the room.

Jordan wasted no time; his tone was one of authority. 'Listen up, we've got new orders from above. You need to get Tommy and Lizzie back to Caister Camp Halt as soon as possible and make sure they board a train to Liverpool Street. You and Watson might as well accompany them for their safety. Keep your eyes peeled for any suspicious activity.' He paused, letting his words sink in before adding, 'This is still a delicate situation, Davis. We can't afford any slip-ups. Understood?'

Davis grunted in acknowledgement, the sound of rustling papers audible in the background. 'Understood, Sir. What about their belongings? Should we pack everything up?' His voice held a hint of uncertainty, reflecting the sudden change in plans.

'Don't worry about that,' Jordan replied, his voice firm and reassuring. 'Clayton, Watts, and I will handle it. We'll collect their things and drive them back to Tooley Street. Just focus on getting those kids to the station safely and without drawing attention.' He paused, then added, 'Remember, discretion is key here. We don't want to raise any suspicions.'

With the plan set in motion, Jordan hung up and headed back to the Caister Holiday Park. There, he briefed Clayton and Watts. They were on the road within the hour, heading towards Rallison's farm to gather Tommy and Lizzie's possessions. The countryside blurred past their windows as they drove at speed.

Meanwhile, Davis and Watson relayed the new instructions to Tommy and Lizzie at the farm. The young couple exchanged worried glances but knew better than to argue. They quickly packed what they could carry, their movements hurried and slightly clumsy in their haste. As they stuffed clothes and personal items into bags, Lizzie's hands trembled slightly, betraying her nervousness. Tommy placed a reassuring hand on her shoulder, his face a mask of concern. They bid a hasty farewell to Farmer Rallison, who stood waving goodbye in the doorway of his farmhouse, his weathered face creased with worry as he watched the young couple prepare to leave.

The journey to Caister Camp Halt was tense and silent, the air thick with unspoken worries and fears. As they boarded the train to Liverpool Street Station, Tommy couldn't shake the persistent, gnawing feeling that they were running again, always one step ahead of an unseen threat that seemed to loom more prominent with each passing moment. The weight of their hastily packed bags felt like a physical manifestation of their anxiety.

As the train lurched forward and pulled away from the platform with a screech of metal on metal, a familiar face appeared in their compartment. It was the conductor who had checked their tickets on their initial journey to Caister Camp Halt, his weathered face creased with the same friendly smile they remembered. His eyes widened in recognition as he took in the young couple and their infant son.

'Well, if it isn't the young couple with the wee babe,' he said, his voice warm with surprise and a hint of curiosity. 'Heading back to London already? Have you enjoyed our wonderful sea air?'

Lizzie nodded, forcing a nervous smile. She unconsciously tightened her grip on James, who slumbered peacefully in her arms, blissfully unaware of the tension surrounding him. 'Yes, our convalescence is over, so we're off,' she replied, her voice steady despite the tremor she felt inside. 'It was a lovely break, but home life calls.'

The conductor's keen gaze swept across the compartment, settling on Watson, who sat stiffly across from the young couple. Sensing the growing tension and the need for a plausible explanation, Tommy quickly interjected, his mind racing to concoct a believable story. 'This is Lizzie's uncle,' he said smoothly, gesturing towards Watts with a casual wave of his hand. 'He's accompanying us back to London. The other guy's his mate.' Tommy's voice carried just the right amount of nonchalance, as if it were the most natural thing in the world for Lizzie's relatives to join them on their journey.

After catching on to Tommy's improvisation, Watts nodded politely to the conductor. His face arranged into a mask of avuncular concern as he added, 'Just making sure my niece and her family get home safe and sound.' The convincing smile he offered seemed to radiate genuine familial warmth.

The conductor's suspicious expression softened, apparently satisfied with this explanation. He gave a curt nod and moved on to check other passengers' tickets, his footsteps fading as he made his way down the narrow aisle of the carriage. As he disappeared from view, Tommy, Lizzie, Davis and Watson exchanged relieved glances, their tense postures relaxing ever so slightly. A moment of shared nervous energy passed between them before they all burst into quiet laughter, the kind born of relief and shared conspiracy.

Chapter 30

Back at Tooley Street

In Bellinger's office, Tommy and Lizzie sat side by side, their shoulders touching for mutual support, with baby James nestled securely in Lizzie's arms. The infant's soft cooing provided a stark contrast to the tense atmosphere. Constable George Turner stood nearby, his sturdy frame and familiar presence offering a silent reassurance to the young couple. His face bore the signs of concern, though he maintained a professional composure.

Detective Inspector Bellinger entered the room with measured steps, his face a complex tapestry of relief and lingering worry. The lines around his eyes seemed more profound than usual, a testament to the strain of recent events. With a weary sigh, he settled into his chair, the leather creaking softly beneath him.

'I've got some news for you,' Bellinger began, his voice steady but tinged with caution. He leaned forward, resting his elbows on the desk. 'The immediate threat we were concerned about has been... resolved. It's a bit of a complicated situation.'

Tommy leaned forward, his brow furrowed in confusion and anticipation. 'What do you mean, resolved? Has something happened?'

Bellinger cleared his throat, his fingers interlacing as he chose his words carefully. 'We've received information from Constable Jordan down at Caister. It appears the individual we were worried about – the one who posed a threat to your family – attempted to flee using a motor launch. Unfortunately for him, the weather took a turn for the worse.'

Lizzie gasped softly, instinctively holding James closer to her chest. The baby squirmed slightly, sensing his mother's tension. Tommy reached out, placing a protective hand on Lizzie's arm.

'The boat was recovered later, minus an anchor and chain,' Bellinger continued, his tone sombre. 'Our best guess, based on the evidence, is that he tried to drop anchor but failed to secure his end properly. The rough seas did the rest – we can only assume he was washed overboard in the turbulent waters.'

Tommy and Lizzie exchanged bewildered glances, their eyes wide as they struggled to process this unexpected turn of events. The room fell silent momentarily, save for the soft clock ticking on Bellinger's office wall.

'We've filed a missing person's report as per procedure, and the local constabulary has been alerted to keep an eye out,' Bellinger added, leaning back in his chair. 'But given the circumstances and the treacherous nature of those waters, it's doubtful he survived the ordeal.'

George shifted uncomfortably, his polished boots squeaking against the floor. His eyes darted between Bellinger and the young couple, gauging their reactions and ready to offer support if needed.

'So... it's over?' Tommy asked hesitantly, his voice barely above a whisper. The words hung in the air, heavy with disbelief and a glimmer of hope.

Bellinger nodded slowly, his expression grave yet tinged with cautious optimism. 'For now, at least. We'll need to remain vigilant – these matters are rarely simple. But yes, the immediate danger that was looming over you has passed. You can breathe a little easier, though we mustn't let our guard down completely.'

Tommy shifted uneasily in his seat, his brow deeply furrowed with concern and his fingers drumming nervously on his thigh. 'What about Liam Dennett? Won't he take his own revenge? He still thinks I had something to do with his brother's murder. The man's not exactly known for his forgiveness.'

Bellinger leaned back in his chair, the old wood creaking softly under his weight. His eyes narrowed as he considered his response.

'We've already thought of that, Tommy. There's a warrant out for his immediate arrest. We're not taking any chances this time.'

Lizzie's eyes widened in surprise, a mix of hope and apprehension flashing across her face. She adjusted her hold on baby James, who stirred slightly in her arms. 'Really? For what exactly? I know he's done plenty, but what's finally tipped the scales?'

'For the brutal beating he gave your father, for one,' Bellinger explained, his tone firm and unwavering. 'Not to mention his terrorist involvement with Malone and the genuine and impending threat he poses to others. The Home Office has given us their consent. No more hanging on waiting to snare the big fish. We're moving forward with full force.'

Tommy's eyebrows shot up, his mouth falling open slightly in disbelief. He leaned forward, his voice dropping to an almost conspiratorial whisper. 'The big fish? You mean... the Dennett Family back in Ireland?'

Bellinger nodded solemnly, his expression grave. 'Not so much the family, their terrorist connections. They probably know now that a key player in their organisation has met with an unfortunate end. It's changed the entire landscape of our operation. The power structure we've been monitoring for months has suddenly shifted in our favour.'

George shifted his weight from one foot to the other, clearing his throat nervously. His eyes darted between Bellinger and Tommy. 'Sir, just to clear, does this mean we're free to pursue Liam Dennett without... interference? No more tiptoeing around?'

'Precisely, George,' Bellinger confirmed, a hint of satisfaction in his voice. 'We're no longer constrained by the need to use him as bait. Our priority now is to bring him in and end this sorry affair. It's time we closed this chapter for good.'

Tommy exhaled slowly, the tension in his shoulders visibly easing. He ran a hand through his hair, his mind racing with the implications. 'So, what happens now? For us, I mean? Are we still in danger?'

Bellinger leaned forward, his elbows resting on his knees as his eyes met Tommy's. His voice was steady and reassuring. 'For now, you and your family will remain under our protection. We can't risk Liam making a move before we apprehend him. But I want you to know, Tommy, that we're doing everything possible to resolve this situation quickly. You've been through enough already.'

Lizzie cradled James closer to her chest, her voice barely above a whisper as she looked down at her sleeping child. 'How long do you think it will take? We've been living in fear for so long... I just want it to be over.'

Bellinger looked at Lizzie with a stern face. 'Maybe it is.' he said, his voice softening as he reached for the telephone on his desk and dialled a number. After what seemed like an eternity, his posture straightened abruptly, tension visibly leaving his shoulders.

'Tommy, Lizzie,' he said, his voice softening as he covered the mouthpiece with his broad hand, 'someone wishes to speak with you. I believe you'll want to take this call.'

Tommy and Lizzie exchanged curious glances, a mixture of apprehension and hope flickering across their faces. Bellinger handed over the receiver, his eyes crinkling with the hint of a smile. Tommy took it gingerly, holding it between them so Lizzie could listen in as well. Their heads were close together in a picture of unity.

'Hello?' Tommy ventured cautiously, his voice barely above a whisper.

'Tommy! Lizzie! It's Lillo,' came the familiar voice, warm and pleasant despite the crackle and hiss of the connection. Their friend's voice sounded like a burst of sunshine on a cloudy day. A smile spread across Tommy's face, starting small and growing until it lit up his entire countenance. It was mirrored perfectly by Lizzie's expression of pleasant surprise, her eyes sparkling with delight.

Lillo's voice continued, filled with genuine affection that seemed to bridge the miles between them. 'I wanted to wish you both the very best of luck for the future. You've been through so much, more than anyone should have, and you deserve all the happiness in the world. I mean that from the bottom of my heart.'

Tommy swallowed hard, a lump forming in his throat as he was touched by Lillo's heartfelt words. 'Thank you, Lillo,' he managed, his voice thick with emotion. 'We can't express how grateful we are for everything you've done. You've been a true friend when we needed one most.'

'No need for thanks,' Lillo insisted, his voice warm and reassuring. 'That's what friends are for, after all. In fact, I have an offer for you both, something I've been thinking about for a while now. You're welcome to come back and stay with us anytime. And if you'd fancy it, there's work for you at Caister Holiday Park next summer. We'd give you your chalet right by the sea, and of course, you'd be paid for your work. It's not much, but it's honest work in a place where you can breathe easy.'

Lizzie's eyes widened, a mix of disbelief and hope shining in them, and she leaned closer to the receiver, her shoulder pressing against Tommy's. 'Really? You'd do that for us, Lillo? After everything that's happened?'

'Of course!' Lillo chuckled, the sound warm and reassuring. 'You're practically family now, both of you. Think about it, eh? No pressure, but the offer's there if you want it. We'd be honoured to have you with us.'

Tommy and Lizzie looked at each other, a spark of hope in their eyes growing stronger with each passing second. For the first time in what felt like an eternity, they allowed themselves to imagine a future filled with possibility rather than fear. The weight of their recent trials seemed to lift, if only for a moment, as they contemplated this unexpected lifeline thrown their way by a friend who had already given them so much.

The Earl of Derby pub on Grange Road buzzed with lunchtime activity, the air thick with the acrid smell of the nearby leather and glue factories. Patrons chatted animatedly over pints and simple meals, their voices creating a lively din that filled the cosy establishment. The clinking of glasses and the occasional burst of laughter punctuated the steady hum of conversation. Staff weaved through the crowded tables, balancing trays laden with steaming plates of pub fare. In one corner, a group of factory workers on their lunch break argued good-naturedly about the Lions' latest football match, while at the bar, a few regulars nursed their drinks and swapped stories with the bartender.

A fleet of vehicles silently pulled up outside the Earl of Derby pub. Several police cars, their bells disengaged, lined the curb. Alongside them, unmarked vehicles disgorged plainclothes officers who moved with purpose and precision. The afternoon air was thick with tension, and a few passers-by quickened their steps, sensing the gravity of the situation unfolding before them.

Detective Inspector Bellinger stood at the centre of the gathering force, his voice low but authoritative as he addressed the team. Officers clustered around him, their faces set with determination. 'Right, listen up, everybody,' Bellinger said, eyes scanning the group. 'On my mark, take every entrance as we discussed. Everybody fit?' He paused, allowing his gaze to linger on each officer, silently assessing their readiness for the task at hand. A chorus of nods and murmured affirmations rippled through the assembled officers. Some adjusted their gear, double-checking holsters and equipment, while others exchanged meaningful glances with their partners. 'OK, everybody, get ready!' Bellinger commanded, his voice carrying the weight of years of experience and authority. The team sprang into action, moving swiftly and silently towards the entrances. They fanned out, covering each possible exit. Uniformed officers took positions at the main entrance, their hands hovering near their truncheons, while plainclothes detectives slipped around to the side and rear doors, blending into the shadows cast by the building.

Inside the pub, patrons remained oblivious to the operation unfolding outside. The clinking of glasses and the hum of conversation continued unabated, a stark contrast to the tense silence of the officers waiting just beyond the doors. Laughter erupted from a corner table, unaware of the impending disruption to the lunchtime's revelry.

Bellinger watched his team take their positions, his hand poised to give the final signal. The air crackled with anticipation as the officers waited, muscles taut and ready to act at their commander's word. He took a deep breath, steeling himself for the moment of truth that was about to unfold.

Then he gave the word to go.

The pub doors burst open simultaneously with a resounding crash, startling the unsuspecting patrons and shattering the jovial atmosphere. Pints sloshed over the rims of glasses, spilling amber liquid onto tabletops and laps. Animated conversations halted mid-sentence, leaving words hanging in the air like unfinished melodies. Heads whipped around in unison, eyes wide with shock and curiosity as they gawked at the sudden commotion. In the ensuing chaos, several plainclothes officers, followed by uniformed men, their faces set with grim determination, zeroed in on a solitary man hunched over at the far end of the bar.

The target, a burly figure with a sullen expression, quickly realised he was cornered. His eyes darted frantically, searching for an escape route that didn't exist. He lashed out with wild, uncoordinated swings in a desperate bid for freedom. His meaty fists connected with an officer's jaw with a sickening crunch, sending the lawman staggering backwards. But the element of surprise quickly faded as more officers closed in. A polished truncheon swung high, catching the target on the side of his head with a dull thud. The impact sent him reeling, doubling him over and causing him to stumble against the bar, knocking over several empty glasses.

Jordan dived into the affray, his muscular frame colliding with Liam's as he wrestled the struggling man to the sticky pub floor. With swift, practised efficiency, Jordan snapped the thick, metal handcuffs around Liam's wrists with a satisfying click. 'Liam Dennett, you're under arrest,' he announced, recovering his breath. Blood trickled from a gash on Liam's forehead, staining his dishevelled hair as Jordan hauled him to his knees with a grunt of effort. The Irishman swayed unsteadily, his eyes unfocused from the blow he'd received. 'Now, if you'd be kind enough to follow these police officers outside and get into one of their vehicles, they've arranged a lift for you to Tooley Street,' Jordan said, his tone calm and polite, a stark contrast to the violence that had just been witnessed. He turned his head, smiling, catching Davis's eye. 'Read him his rights, would you? There's a good chap,' he instructed, maintaining his professional bearing despite the adrenaline still pumping through his veins.

Davis's face split into a wide grin, a glint of satisfaction in his eyes. 'Whatever you say, boss,' he quipped, a hint of playful sarcasm in his voice. Davis and another officer grabbed Liam by his collar and forcefully dragged him face down towards the pub exit, his feet frantically scrambling for purchase on the worn, beer-stained floorboards. His legs flailed wildly, knocking against tables and chairs as he struggled against their iron grip. One of his scuffed leather shoes caught on a rickety barstool, the laces snagging and coming loose. The shoe remained behind a lone testament to the violent scuffle that had just unfolded. It lay there, upturned and forlorn, a silent witness to Liam's desperate attempts to evade capture as he was dragged out of the pub doorway and into the street.

One by one, the officers rushed from the pub, their boots thundering across the worn floorboards as they followed Liam and his two captors. The heavy oak pub door swung shut with a resounding thud, the brass hinges creaking in protest. Outside, engines roared to life, and the convoy of police vehicles systematically gunned up

Grange Road, their tyres screeching against the damp asphalt. The cacophony of police bells grew fainter and fainter until they faded into the distance, leaving the Earl of Derby in a state of stunned silence. Patrons exchanged wide-eyed glances, their drinks forgotten on tables and bar tops, condensation forming rings on the polished wood. Pints of ale were left untouched as the regulars tried to process the whirlwind of violence that had invaded their local. The air hung heavy with tension and the lingering scent of fear, mixed with stale beer and cigarette smoke. Hushed whispers began to ripple through the crowd as shock slowly gave way to a burning curiosity about the dramatic events that had unfolded before their eyes.

Chapter 31

August Bank Holiday

Police Constable George Turner pedalled his bicycle along Tooley Street, his weatherproof gear keeping him almost dry as the rain pelted down relentlessly. It was Monday, August 2nd, Bank Holiday, and the weather was living up to its reputation with a vengeance. George's uniform clung to him, damp despite his best efforts, as he navigated the puddle-strewn road, his tyres sending up sprays of water with each revolution. As he approached Parson's Fields, George slowed his bicycle, the wheels splashing through shallow pools of rainwater that reflected the grey sky above. He dismounted with practised ease, leaning the bike against the remains of the cast iron fence that had seen better days. Just as he settled into his usual spot, a miraculous change swept over the area. The clouds parted as if by divine intervention, allowing a shaft of bright sunlight to burst through, illuminating the fields in a golden glow that seemed almost otherworldly after the dreary morning.

Soon, the sudden warmth caused steam to rise from the wet grass and pavement, creating a misty, almost ethereal atmosphere that transformed the mundane street into something out of a fairy tale. As if on cue, the doors of the St. John's Tavern swung open with a creak, and people began to emerge, blinking in the unexpected sunshine like moles emerging from their burrows. Antonio, ever the opportunist with an uncanny sense of timing, cranked up his music machine, the cheerful melody cutting through the post-rain silence and adding a festive air to the scene. The world seemed to spring back to life, shaking off the gloom of the earlier downpour like a dog shaking water from its coat.

George's keen eyes were drawn to a gathering outside the pub, a splash of colour and movement against the still-damp backdrop. There, amid the impromptu celebration, he spotted Tommy and Lizzie Baker, with little James bouncing excitedly in his mother's arms, his chubby hands seemingly reaching for the sunbeams. Jack and Harriet were there too, the older couple's faces creased with smiles, all swaying to the lively tunes from Antonio's machine. Their faces were alight with joy, the troubles of recent months momentarily forgotten in this unexpected burst of Bank Holiday cheer.

A smile tugged at George's lips as he watched the scene unfold, feeling a warmth in his chest that had little to do with the emerging sun. He reached into his pocket, pulling out a cigarette and lighting it with practised ease, the flame from his Ronson briefly illuminating his weathered features. As he took a long, satisfying drag, he leaned back against the fence, savouring the moment and the rich Woodbine taste. The smoke curled lazily in the humid air as George mused, his eyes twinkling with amusement and a touch of fondness for the community he served and protected. As he watched the impromptu celebration, George felt a renewed sense of purpose and a deep appreciation for the resilience of the human spirit.

'You know,' he murmured to himself, his voice barely audible above the music and laughter, 'this ain't such a bad place after all.'

The End

Acknowledgements

My gratitude extends to Anita Ibanez MA for outstanding artwork as always.

To Ignatius Hughes KC for his assistance and direction with the evolution of the IRA and recent Irish history leading up to the period covering the 1940s and 1950s.

With gratitude to Stuart Amesbury for his invaluable insight, analytical skill, and thoughtful suggestions which enhanced the accuracy, chronology, and structure of the storyline.

Notes from the Author

The Camp Song

The inspiration for the title of this novel comes from the first line of the song that was regularly sung at the start of meals at holiday camps during the 1950s.

Always eat when you are hungry
Always drink when you are dry
Close your eyes when you are sleepy
Don't stop breathing or you'll die
Ahhhhhh...men!

Nobody took the religious implications of this song seriously. What they did take seriously, and embraced wholeheartedly, was the real sense of comradeship that singing this song installed in all those seated in the camp dining room.

Once the singing was over the dining room rang with clatter of catering trolleys and the clinking of plates. There was always a soup and bread roll starter for lunch and dinner (or as it was known '*dinner and tea*') for which the men were regularly chastised by their wives for breaking the roll up into small pieces, floating them in the soup then dunking each piece prior to slurping it all up. Wives would strive to deploy the '*posh*' way of spooning the soup which involved tipping the bowl away from them, pushing the spoon through the soup before scooping up a spoonful from the far edge of the bowl. This often resulted with the soup washing over the far edge and ending up on the table cloth due to the wives complete lack of practice of this etiquette when at home. The men however, held on no such ceremony, adopting an '*elbows up and get on with it*' approach to the task ahead.

The IRA in the 1950s

'*Operation Harvest*' was the first major military undertaking carried out by the IRA since the 1940s, when the harsh security measures of both the Republic of Ireland and Northern Ireland governments had severely weakened it. In 1939-40 the IRA carried out a sabotage/bombing campaign in England (the S-Plan) to try to force British withdrawal from Northern Ireland. From 1942 to 1944 it also mounted an ineffective campaign in Northern Ireland. Internment on both sides of the border, as well as internal feuding and disputes over future policy, all but destroyed the organisation. These campaigns were officially called off on 10 March 1945. By 1947, the IRA had only 200 activists, according to its own general staff.

In 1948 a General Army Convention issued General Order No. 8, prohibiting 'any armed action whatsoever' against the forces of the recently proclaimed Republic of Ireland, amounting to a de facto recognition of the state. Under the new policy, IRA volunteers who were caught with arms in the Republic of Ireland were ordered to dump or destroy them and not to take defensive action. From then on, armed action was focused on Northern Ireland. In 1954, after an arms raid at Gough Barracks in Armagh, a speaker at the Wolfe Tone commemoration at Bodenstown confirmed that IRA policy was directed solely against British forces in Northern Ireland. By the middle of this decade, moreover, the IRA had substantially re-armed. This was achieved by means of arms raids launched between 1951 and 1954, on British military bases in Northern Ireland and England.

[:: *source Wikipedia - Border campaign (Irish Republican Army)* ::]

Italian POWs in Norfolk

POW camps were common across Norfolk, popping up in areas where work was needed most. Pudding Norton camp was built in the early

1940s to house Italian and later, German and Ukrainian prisoners of war. One POW camp was based at Hempton Green, Hempton, Fakenham. In 1947 around 8,000 men were brought to Great Britain from a POW enclave in Rimini, Italy. On arriving in Britain the POWs were split up and sent to several different camps the largest number going to Hempton Green which housed 1001, later this number reduced to around 875.

Norfolk people opened up their homes and their hearts for Italian and German POWs for Christmas. It seems strange that a wartime enemy would be invited over to Christmas so soon after the war – but this was the case across Norfolk. Few realise just how significant these people were in Britain, particularly agricultural areas such as Norfolk, where they were largely used as labourers. In Norfolk, the sight of Italian POWs working the land would have been a common one, as they proved vital to aiding the recovery of the crippled British economy following the war. For example, the winter was cold and bitter in 1947, and many country roads throughout Norfolk were blocked with snow. Clearing it was a task which was vital to complete, and many PoWs were called out to deal with it.

There was very little anger from the locals towards prisoners, and by 1948, the majority of them had been repatriated to their homes.

Caister-on-Sea Holiday Park

Caister Holiday Park first opened in 1906 and is the oldest holiday centre in the UK. It was set up by John Fletcher Dodd, a former grocer and a founder member of the Independent Labour Party, as a socialist holiday camp to offer cheap holidays and breaks to the working people of East London. During the 1930s the holiday camp built the largest dance hall for miles around - it was big enough to accommodate 600 couples on the dance floor! A new dining hall was also built that could seat 500 people.

The 1950s Caister Holiday Park became a real family holiday camp with upgraded accommodation and a choice of bars and entertainment. So many people now wanted to experience a seaside holiday at Caister that the former Midland and Great Northern Railway laid on a special summer Saturday express train from Liverpool Steet called the '*Down Holiday Camps Express*'. This ran from London to Caister-on-Sea via Cambridge, Ely, Norwich and Wroxham until the line and station closed in 1959. The railway station was originally called Caister Camp Halt.

[:: excerpt taken from caistercaravan.co.uk
The History of Caister Holiday Park ::]

August Bank Holiday

The August Bank Holiday or Summer Bank Holiday is a public holiday in the United Kingdom, part of the statutory bank holiday provision. Originally, the holiday was held on the first Monday of August across the country, but was changed in the late 1960s to the last Monday in August for England, Wales and Northern Ireland. It remains the first Monday for Scotland.

In 1964, an experimental move to the end of August was announced by the Secretary of State for Industry, Trade and Regional Development, Edward Heath, taking effect for two years from 1965, responding to pressure from the holiday industry to extend the season. The move applied to England and Wales, but not to Scotland.

Following the two year trial, each year's date was announced in Parliament on an ad hoc basis, causing problems for publishers of the calendars and diaries. The rule seems to have been to select the weekend of the last Saturday in August, so that in 1968 and 1969 Bank Holiday Monday actually fell in September, causing concern amongst some politicians.

The date was settled in statute with the passage of the Banking and Financial Dealings Act 1971, which remains in force today, with the date specified as "the last Monday in August".

[:: source Wikipedia – August Bank Holiday ::]

Adult Content (Strong Language)

I hesitated to edit out the strong language which largely prevails in Act One of this novel but in the end chose instead to include it for the reason that strong language was commonplace and a part of daily life in Bermondsey and the docks at the time of the storyline.

Coming Soon

The Kitsune and The Hatamoto is a fantasy set in medieval, feudal Japan. The Kitsune, a shape-shifting fox revered in Japanese folk lore, seeks revenge for the death of his father by a young Samurai warrior bent on fox hunting, a practice banned by the Feudal Lords for the disrespecting a deity. The reader follows the journey of the young fox and his transformation to Kitsune, at which point the tables turn on the young Samurai, now a Hatamoto, guardian of the flag and loyal officer to the Feudal Lord.

Also available from Leonard John

Love Poetry – a short collection of poems for lovers and lovers of life

*Now available
from tradshack.com*

A final thank you

Thank you dear reader for taking the time to read my novel. I hope it was an enjoyable experience.

If it was I would really appreciate it if you left a comment on my publishing site TradShack.

Here's the link:

https://tradshack.com/product/always-eat-when-you-are-hungry/

Bless you!
Leonard John